STOPOVER STORIES

STOPOVER STORIES

Duncan Delaporte

The Book Guild Ltd.

Sussex, England.

The Book Guild Ltd.
25 High Street,
Lewes, Sussex.

First published 1991
© Duncan Delaporte 1991
Set in Baskerville
Typesetting by Southern Reproductions (Sussex)
East Grinstead, Sussex.
Printed in Great Britain by
Antony Rowe Ltd.
Chippenham, Wiltshire.

British Library Cataloguing in Publication Data
Delaporte, Duncan
  Stopover stories
  I. Title
  823.914 [F]

ISBN 0 86332 593 9

*International business travel
isn't always a pleasure
but it is a privilege.
These stories have been
written about those travels
over many years and
countries.*

*To Rita, Christian and Nadia
who put up with my
many stopovers.*

CONTENTS

Normandy
———————Beach Head———————

MONSIEUR BRESSE sighed contentedly to himself and leaned across for the third time in ten minutes to polish his hotel's reception counter. A tall thin man with an even thinner face he pursed his lips, ran his hand through a full head of slightly greying hair and sighed again.

He could well be proud of himself, he thought. Seven years ago this same counter had been neglected and scarred, now it was restored and cherished. It was some seven years he mused since he and his wife Marie-Anne had made the decision to leave their native Paris, and buy a hotel in Normandy. He recalled the laughter and derision of his Parisian friends when they had announced their intention. Why do you two who have lived in Paris all your lives, want to become seaside hoteliers? You must be mad, it's a farming area, full of Calvados and cows. You'll be back, they'd all said, and soon.

It was true though, that during the first few years it hadn't been easy. He'd had his doubts, that was for sure. They'd wanted to go up the coast to Deauville, which at least had had some sort of reputation, if only that of a left over from the *Belle Epoque*. Alas, the legacy, left by his father, had not stretched to the prices asked in that resort for the type of property he was looking for. He and Marie-Anne had to settle for something down the coast at Granville. It had been a sleepy little fishing village, a backwater between its grander neighbour and the tourist attractions of Mont St Michelle further south. It just hadn't any real image or tradition. Then he smiled again, but what it had had was the three P's, Position, Potential and Prestige. These three magic words had been given to him by his father, whose dream it had been to be his own boss rather than work as he had done for years as the head waiter at the Café Royal. His father had painted a

9

glowing image of the aristocracy whom he waited on but longed really to serve. The seeds had been planted.

When he and Marie-Anne had first come out of the station at Granville and seen opposite the Auberge de la Gare, they had been dismayed. It had been big, going to rack and ruin, it looked so sad in the rain, but Monsieur Bresse had not been put off. It fulfilled the three P's, next to the station, run down and under-developed, and beneath the tatty exterior he could see the Edwardian facade and the splendour that might be. They'd bought it quickly and cheaply which was just as well, because they had had to pour every franc they made into it over the next two years to restore it to its former glory. To do that, and he shuddered remembering, they'd take any trade going during that period, anyone, but anyone was welcome. Monsieur Bresse wrinkled his nose as he recalled some of the clients. Railway workers, who'd been regulars for years, drinking before, after and sometimes during the day. Travelling salesmen, who'd tried to make up to Marie-Anne. Illicit lovers, who'd arrived late on Friday nights, and rushed across the road to the first hotel they'd seen. He'd had them all he recalled, but no more.

Now it had all changed and soon the very symbols of his good fortune, and hard work he hastily reminded himself, would be arriving for their fourth annual holiday at the Auberge. He stopped dead and glanced at his watch. They would soon be here. He rushed across to the dining room and looked in to see Henri, the head waiter of the past three years, giving the glassware in the dining salon a final polish, before lunch. Henri looked up and Monsieur Bresse nodded approvingly, but not too familiarly, in the style of the *Grand Patron,* he imagined himself to be.

This salon was his pride and joy. The bar which had housed the local riff-raff had been done away with and transformed into a magnificent dining room. Henri now presided with two assistant waiters over a restaurant which could seat up to forty, and which, over the years, had built up quite a reputation in the town and surrounding countryside.

The thought made Monsieur Bresse smile again; now they were looked up to in the town. They, more than anyone, liked to think they were the ones who had been responsible for changing Granville's image from that of a sleepy fishing village to that of a charming stopover and newly-discovered seaside resort on the

Normandy coast. They had also transformed the Auberge into the regular haunt of the local upper classes and the premier hotel in town.

This had been confirmed when the Burnham-Jones's from England had arrived four years ago to stay with them. They had swept into town in their Rolls-Royce and caused a sensation, staying for three weeks, and they had returned annually since then. Every year the Bresses welcomed them with open arms. Nothing, but nothing, was too much trouble for the Burnham-Jones's. They had the best rooms in the house, the Emperor Suite, created from one double and two small singles on the top floor. It was the only room with a sea view, and Marie-Anne had lavishly furnished it. A little overdone perhaps, he thought, but on the whole in good taste.

Marie-Anne appeared. 'Have they arrived yet?' she asked, 'they are late. Their telegram said they'd be here for lunch, and it is nearly twelve already.' She was nervous, thought Monsieur Bresse, and gazed at his wife fondly. She was thin like him, but she knew how to dress. Not for her the local seamstresses. No, four times a year she went off to Paris and came back well equipped for the next three months. He didn't mind, indeed it had added to their reputation locally and, now they were accepted, it was even more important to keep up appearances.

'No, no, ma chérie, don't worry they'll be here.'

Marie-Anne relaxed a little, and made her way into the salon to check up yet again on the table flowers she had arranged earlier. Monsieur Bresse nodded contentedly and went back behind the counter to wait.

The restaurant was full, the hotel was full. Monsieur Bresse was content. It had been a busy week, the height of the season, they had been rushed off their feet. But it had been and was a great success! The Burnham-Jones's were really enjoying themselves. They had turned up last Saturday at just gone twelve, and been welcomed with open arms.

Mr Burnham-Jones had not changed a bit Monsieur Bresse had said. Still the distinguished looking ex-military man. Ramrod back, square shoulders and the short back and sides haircut, so beloved of the English. Mrs Burnham-Jones had hugged Marie-Anne and kissed her on both cheeks with obvious affection. Marie-Anne particularly liked studying her wardrobe.

She was always well dressed in the English country style which secretly Marie-Anne wanted to emulate but was never able to with her waspish figure. The Burnham-Jones's had spoken to them in their broken French, which was a ritual until the Bresses, with many compliments to the improvements since the previous year, switched to English. They loved, particularly in front of their other guests, to show off their talents. Monsieur Bresse had even used it as an example to the local Chamber of Commerce. Granville should move with the times, he'd pronounced, indeed the local college had started English evening classes, to which he proudly sent his junior waiters, another example of what he had done for the town. That was the trouble with the locals; they had no sense of progress.

The Burnham-Jones's had in turn complimented them on the little improvements to the Auberge since last year and Marie-Anne was glad that she'd recovered the couches and chairs in the Emperor Suite.

The Burnham-Jones's had been busy the whole week, shopping, travelling all over town, making their presence felt in the bars and cafés, and each lunch time and evening returning to dine in the salon, attentively waited on by Henri, even if they did, conservative English that they were, stick to the fixed menu. The tradespeople who called at the hotel all mentioned their special guests, and the Bresses knew that wherever the Rolls went, people would know who its occupants were and where they were staying.

They were presently in the dining room enjoying their lunch, and Monsieur Bresse was ensconced behind the counter pushing bits of paperwork this way and that. He looked up suddenly as the front door crashed open. He frowned as he saw a young man with a rucksack push through the opening. The plastic sandals, dirty jeans and khaki shirt did not make a good impression on Monsieur Bresse. The rucksack was off the shoulder and the young man was now making his way over to the desk. Monsieur Bresse was making his way out to show him the door as quickly as possible. He, at the same time, spoke quickly, 'Monsieur,' he said, 'this is the Auberge, you were looking for directions perhaps?' He hastily added, 'My hotel is full Monsieur.'

The young man smiled. He was used to dealing with hoteliers and in perfect French replied. 'I have come,' he said, 'Monsieur, to meet Mr Burnham-Jones, who I believe, is a guest at your hotel.' Monsieur Bresse was a little shocked, but he quickly recovered his composure.

'Yes,' he said 'really, I will inform Mr Burnham-Jones that you are here.' He strode into the dining room and called Henri over. 'Tell Mr Burnham-Jones' he said and gestured, 'someone has asked for him.'

He returned to the hall and saw that the young man had sat down and was hand rolling a cigarette. Amazing, he thought, there must be some mistake. Any illusions on that score were swiftly dismissed as Mr Burnham-Jones rushed into the hall and greeted the young man warmly. Mr Burnham-Jones turned to Monsieur Bresse, 'Michael,' he said, 'will be joining us for lunch, would you be so kind as to store his things please?'

Monsieur Bresse smiled uneasily, but took the proffered rucksack gingerly and put it behind the counter. He was intrigued and much bothered. Marie-Anne and he had made strict rules about dress in the salon, and he could see that one or two of the diners were looking up strangely at the new arrival. Still, what could he do, unless he upset his favourite guests? Marie-Anne appeared and he gestured and explained what had happened, and the dilemma. She too was upset, but agreed that there was nothing they could do about it for the present.

An hour passed and almost everyone had left the salon. Monsieur Bresse was sure that some of the diners had left a little earlier than usual, and certainly it was difficult to see that anyone could have ignored the laughter and noise coming from the company at the Burnham-Jones's table since the guest had arrived.

Finally, after a round of cognac, they rose, Mrs Burnham-Jones a little unsteadily, and made their way out. They shook hands with Michael and Monsieur Bresse quickly brought the rucksack round. He was going, thank God. Michael hugged and kissed Mrs Burnham-Jones, slapped Mr Burnham-Jones on the back and spoke. 'I'll see you at home then,' he said, 'I'll tell Mum and Dad you'll pick them up at the usual place and time. Lovely to see you.' He turned and with a grin at Monsieur Bresse, went out of the doors and across the road to the station.

Mr and Mrs Burnham-Jones stood there watching him go, then turned to Monsieur Bresse. 'Such a nice boy,' said Mrs Burnham-Jones, 'always said he'd drop by and see us one year. It's only a short way from Deauville.'

'Splendid lunch,' said Mr Burnham-Jones, 'Michael said it's even better than they get in the Grand.'

Monsieur Bresse knew that there was only one Grand on the coast. That boy staying at the Grand! 'I'm so glad,' Monsieur Bresse said. 'Is he a friend of yours?'

'Friend, well I suppose you could say that,' said Mr Burnham-Jones, 'actually, he's our employer's son.'

Monsieur Bresse's mouth opened. 'Your employer?' he said.

'Yes, our employer,' said Mr Burnham-Jones. 'We always drop his Mother and Father at the Grand, then we come down here. They're very good to us really, let us have the same time off as them and let us take the car. Not everyone would do that for their chauffeur and housekeeper nowadays, I can tell you.'

Covering
─────── The Waterfront ───────

I'D JUST FINISHED at the Plaza, our New York headquarters on the east side of Manhattan. It had been a long hard day. The constant hassle of this highly competitive town extended off the sidewalk, and up the escalators and lifts into the fabric of every one of the forty nine floors of our sky-scraper. As an intermittent visitor from the UK, I could take it or leave it. Today I'd been taking it, and now I was glad to be leaving it.

The evening stretched before me. All my own, I had plans: a taxi to the hotel downtown, a shower, then out to the west side to a little Italian restaurant I'd found the other day. I didn't want to hear any more crap about corporate strategy, goals and all the rest of the jargon, which was what our senior blue-suited, conservatively spoken demi-god management was spouting these days. An evening relaxing away from them all, then tomorrow back to London and civilization.

I looked down the street; there were no taxis. Why is it in any town in the world when you don't need a taxi there are hundreds of them, and when you do, there are never any about? I sighed, and started walking towards Wall Street, sure that I'd be able to find one there. It was a sultry, late autumn evening, and the humidity was high. I could feel my shirt sticking to my body and tiny rivulets of sweat started to form on my forehead. Christ! I needed a taxi and a drink. But which was the stronger need? The desire for a drink won and I started looking for a bar.

There weren't many in that part of town but as I got down to the Fishermen's wharf, I recalled seeing an old tavern next to the docks and I made my way in the rough direction of my memory. Sure enough, on the corner of the block opposite the fish market was the bar. The Ship's Tavern; original I thought, as I pushed open the swing doors and savoured the blast from the cool air-conditioned interior.

The bar itself was long, about thirty feet, and I could just make out in the dimly lit interior, a number of crowded shapes huddled over their drinks. As my eyes got used to the gloom, I realised I'd made a mistake. This wasn't a bar, it was a dive! Too late, I realised people were looking round to see what had come in. This was obviously a place no businessman would go. Old soaks abounded. My throat was parched, what the hell, I'd stay and have just one quick beer. I wondered about my American colleagues up the road. They'd probably be ensconced in their trendy cocktail lounges in the World Trade Centre, and I'd be here with the real world. I'd assert my independence from the corporate machine. Pathetic really, I thought, but I would have that beer.

By now the heads that had turned were no longer interested, so I strolled in, in what I thought was a nonchalant fashion. I made my way to the bar and sat down on a stool that had seen better days. The barman, a fat-necked, open-shirted guy with a filthy apron on, sauntered over.

'What'll it be?' he asked, looking me over with paunchy lidded red veined eyes.

'A Budweizer,' I said.

'What's that again?' he queried, leaning forward in a threatening manner.

'A Budweizer,' I repeated.

Again he looked at me. Then he grinned. 'You mean a Budweezer. You foreign or summit?'

'Well, English actually,' I said.

He laughed out loud. 'Gee a Budweizer for the limey.'

I couldn't tell whether he approved of my being English or not, but the way he said it attracted some attention from the other people in the bar.

'Goddam it, a limey,' he said again as the glass was thrust across at me.

Something stirred beside me and I felt a hand on my shoulder.

'Don't mind Bill,' the voice said, 'he don't like anyone, let alone a limey.' I looked at the person addressing me as he proffered his hand. 'Pete Robinson,' he said, 'of English stock, way back, and proud of it.' I guessed he was about sixty years old, beaten old face, greying hair, twinkling blue eyes, wearing blue denim jacket and jeans, standard uniform of the American working man, still all there, I thought, despite obviously having had a few drinks.

'Hi,' I said. He moved onto the stool next to me.

'Have another beer,' and he beckoned Bill the barman over. 'Give him another Bud, Bill, and one more for me.'

I took the first cold beer and drank it all the way down, savouring the cool bite into the back of my throat, and wondering what I was getting myself into. New York isn't renowned for its friendliness, particularly meeting people in strange bars. I wished I was in the World Trade Centre and then again, wished I wasn't. No, this was OK, a drink with a seemingly friendly stranger.

We chatted away and I warmed to the man. New York bar drinker he may have been but he'd certainly been around as he soon started to tell me.

'Yes,' he said as we downed our second beer together, 'never been to England, but most everywhere else, during the war of course. The islands – I've seen them all. A sailor in the Pacific fleet I was, for most of it. And well you know tonight's a special night, that's why I'm here, kinda anniversary, no – a re-union more like.'

He continued slurring his words a little with the drink but was still sober. 'Last week, after nigh on thirty five years, well, I met my old pal Joey. Yessir, thirty five years, and well tonight, he and I are gonna meet here, and party, and raise hell, just like the old days.'

I smiled to myself, here it comes I thought, an American who's known me for twenty minutes and I'm getting the life history. I listened closely.

'Yeh,' he said, 'my pal Joey. He and I go back a long way. We were stokers together on the *USS Warsprite* back there in '43, shift coal all day long, weeks on end, stuck down in the hold. Never knowed whether you'd be alive one minute to the next, side by side. Near on two years cruising around them islands. So hell, when we could get ashore, we'd raise hell! We'd drink, and drink, and go after them gals. Those were the days, free as a bird, just me and Joey. Hit the high spots, just two good old boys!'

'Another couple beers here, Bill.' He was getting drunker, so I humoured him and listened to the stories of him and his pal Joey. They were quite interesting in a way. Him and old Joey loomed larger than life. I could just see the two of them raising hell in the Pacific.

'Yup,' he said, 'and last week, well there I was taking my cab around the corner, when who the hell do you think I picked up as a fare? Well, it was my old pal Joey!'

Ah, I thought, that's where all the taxis get to, no wonder I hadn't been able to find one. My companion smiled wide-eyed and contented, beaming all over.

'Joey,' he went on, 'didn't look any different than he had in the war. Sure he looked a bit older, who didn't? But I could still see he was a hell raiser! Yup, I could see that and nothing's changed. Well, we arranged to meet this evening here, two old buddies gonna raise hell.' He leaned across, put his arm around my shoulder and winked conspiratorily.

'Yup, I've laid on a couple of broads, and we're gonna hit the town.'

I looked over my shoulder to where he was pointing and sure enough in the corner, looking at us, and probably wondering if I was the Old Pal Joey they'd come to raise hell with, were two middle-aged but not bad looking women. Peroxide blondes, who'd seen better days, cheery faces and cheery smiles.

'Hey,' he said, 'I only came over to get the gals a drink and I've been talking to you all this time.' He glanced at his watch and smiled. 'Any time now Joey comes through them doors.' He slapped his knee in gleeful anticipation, stood up and motioned to Bill the barman.

He shook my hand, wished me well and took the drinks he ordered over to the women. 'Yup,' he said, by way of a parting shot, 'couple of drinks here, then back to my place with the gals, gonna raise hell!'

I envied him. He had a night of laughs and drink and women in front of him. He'd be re-living those days with Joey. All I'd got to look forward to was a quiet dinner and early bed.

'Well,' I said to Bill 'I'd better be going, it's been good, how much do I owe you?'

He shrugged and winked. 'All on Pete.'

I drained the glass and walked over to the table where my friend was. I shook his hand, 'You and Joey, you raise hell!' He guffawed loudly, the women looking embarrassed. I turned around and began walking out.

I pushed open the door and stepped into the street. It was still light, though fading, but after the dark it hurt my eyes. I rubbed them and stepped on the step to the sidewalk while I looked at my watch. I'd been in there nearly an hour and had had a little too much to drink on an empty stomach. Just in front of me, a man and a woman were standing looking up at the bar. Elderly but not old. She had her arm through his. He was looking at a piece of paper. 'Yes,' he said, 'this is it, the Ship's Tavern.'

I made way for them and couldn't help overhearing what they said as I walked away.

'You're gonna like this guy, Julie, we go back a long way. I want him to meet all the family, the kids as well.'

The woman looked up at her husband lovingly, 'Sure thing Joey,' she said, 'anything you say.'

The Perfect
—————Office Junior—————

MIKE JAMES looked up at the Arrivals Board above his head. Scanning it quickly, like the old hand he was, he saw that the British Airways flight had just landed. Perfect timing, he said to himself and, with a grin spread across his face, he strode in the well-mannered gait of an English ex-public schoolboy to the Arrivals Hall. On the way he straightened his tie, and ran his fingers through his sleekly groomed hair. The tropical heat in the poorly air-conditioned building was making him sweat, and he took a handkerchief from his blazer pocket and wiped his brow, replacing it carefully as before.

Despite his grin and buoyancy, he was fed up. Not depressed, not bored, not particularly tired either, just plain pissed off. He'd led a bit of a sheltered life until his assignment in Thailand had started. His mother was English; his father Australian, a pilot who'd come over, inclined in the war to romantic adventures, to fly Spitfires. Mike had been brought up in a typical middle class English town, Sevenoaks, and only a bright brain and a scholarship to a minor English public school had saved him from his father's later fate, an accountant for a city bank. Although he'd not been much good at school, he'd scraped by enough to go to a redbrick university, and had from there with his charm and good manners, sold himself on the university milk round to his present and first employers.

After six months paddling around various departments, trying to learn the business, but more interested in the women than the work, he'd been advised by personnel to put in for an international assignment. A bit wary at first, he'd asked what the alternatives were. On being told that a margarine factory in the north of England wanted a production trainee, and believing, as any right-minded middle-class Englishman from the south would, that this was equivalent to exile, he'd put in for the

22

international side and been sent off to Thailand in the Bangkok regional office.

The only trouble was, he mused to himself, as he pushed through the native throng, was that his sole responsibility for the past eighteen months had been meeting senior management at the airport, settling them into their hotel, conducting them to the office for a short tour and taking them round to enjoy the city's notorious night life.

Old Worthington, the office manager, had explained it succinctly to him on the first day he started.

'Look here, old man,' he'd said, 'nothing much doing out here, just a few local contracts to take care of, that's all. Keep the old paperwork going and you'll be all right. I'll introduce you to the club when you've been here a while. The main thing you have to do is keep our visitors happy. Don't know why we have so many when there's not much going on. Still they keep on coming. All they want is to see the local sights, and a bit of nookie on the side. Too old at my age to drag around, that's why I always put in for a trainee. That's your job for the next four years, keep them happy. Keep your nose clean and I'll give you a good recommendation, so you can wind your way back home when your time's up.'

And that had been it. It was only later he discovered why Worthington couldn't go after the nookie. It wasn't because of his age, it was because of his preferences, which he'd been fully indulging, with the continuous turnover of young local boys in the office, for the fifteen years he'd been in the country. Still, Mike was quite fond of the old sod.

He looked towards the gate and waited. Who was it this time, he thought, and reached inside his pocket for the telex which had arrived the day before. *Simon Eterson, Divisional Vice-President Marketing, Europe, Middle East and Far East, arriving on BA 670 at 2.00 pm from Hong Kong. Please meet and make arrangements for one night stopover. Departs BA 693 to Sydney at 3.00 pm the following day.* A short stay this one, most stopped for two nights, some for three, but he'd never had anyone for longer.

The lights on the board flickered and BA 670 went from 'Landed' to 'IN ARRIVAL'. Mike moved to the back of the hall and gave one of the small children standing with an empty baggage trolley a handful of change. They earned themselves a living that way, grabbing the trolleys early in the morning, and then literally renting them out. He pushed it towards the gate and could see that the passengers from the Hong Kong flight were streaming out.

That looked like him, a rather portly man of about fifty-five, blue pin-striped suit. Would they ever learn, and the Company tie! The man looked anxiously around. Mike James deliberately left him. He'd found it better to let his visitors sweat a bit in the confusion, then when they were getting a bit anxious, he'd rush over and rescue them. They were always more grateful that way. Mike James sprang to attention and went over.

'Mr Eterson, sir, so glad to meet you. Mike James, local office. Bit chaotic, sir, as usual, never mind, car outside, sir, let me take your luggage.'

Eterson nodded, you could see he was used to the red carpet treatment, deferential employees bowing and scraping all over the world. He allowed himself to be led through the terminal and out into the sweltering sun.

The car was already parked in the spot reserved for diplomats. One of the concessions Old Worthington had managed to wangle through his club contacts over the years. Mike loaded the bag in the boot, and then opened the rear side door to let Eterson in. He settled himself in the driving seat and it wasn't until they were well out of the airport that he spoke to his senior colleague. 'I trust sir, that you had a pleasant flight, I've booked a suite for you at the Interconty,' Mike said using a clipped know-it-all tone.

Eterson spoke, 'Thanks er, James,' he said, 'need to rest up for a few hours. Has a programme been arranged? This evening?'

Mike smiled to himself. Always the same, his visitors, looked tired, or feigned tiredness but none of them would make the journey or arrange a trip to stop over in Bangkok for the visit to the local office. Old Worthington had been right. They just wanted a good time. 'Nothing official,' Old Worthington had said, 'whatever they want Mike, you just make sure they get it, strip joint, massage parlour, they like to let their hair down. Then they'll pay us a visit in the morning, quick tour so to speak, then off to the airport and home or on their way. That's why,' Old Worthington had gone on, 'I've been left alone for so long. Doesn't matter what we turn in by way of business, this is their R and R, this is the bit of the trip that the wives never hear about, this is the old nudge and wink to their friends back home. Just make sure you look after them well, that's all. All part of the assignment, Mike.'

It had gone according to schedule so far. Eterson had booked into the hotel, Mike having arranged for a small fee for the manager to greet him, casually of course, that always impressed them. It showed them that the local man, young though he was, knew his way around. Then he'd left him, arranging to pick him up at 7.00 pm. Mike had gone home, changed, and was now sitting in the car outside the hotel waiting for his man. Yes, he could just see him, bang on time. They always were, just like schoolboys eager for the treat. A light suit and sunglasses. My God, thought Mike, that's a new one, he must be keen and guilty, so much the better. Mike made a mental note of this and frowned. He got out and looked at the man, a quarry if ever he saw one. 'Over here, sir, all ready to go.' The older man got quickly into the car, but this time he got in the front not the back.

'Nice to see you, James. Look here,' he suddenly volunteered, 'can't keep calling you "James" all evening, off duty you know. Mike isn't it?'

'Well,' Mike replied, 'if you're quite sure.' He always enjoyed this bit, 'it's Michael actually but Mike is what everyone calls me in the office.'

'Well Mike,' he said, 'what's it to be, dinner and some of the sights, eh?'

'Well, sir,' said Mike 'actually' and this was where he took over, 'I thought you might enjoy a little club I know, rather exclusive, very discreet. Good food, and well an interesting floor show.' There was silence. You could see Eterson thinking. Well, he thought, I haven't come all this way for nothing, and they'd all said back home just how correct the local office junior was. Go to Bangkok, old man, they'd recommended, on your way down under, see the local operation, and there's a damn fine young fellow out there, name of James, he'll look after you. Went to a reasonable school, you know – one of us, knows the ropes, won't let you down.

'Good show,' said Eterson, 'let's relax and enjoy ourselves.' Another one, counted Mike, six out of six, the kid does tricks.

They pulled out of the hotel forecourt. 'I think,' Mike said,

'you'll find the *My Thai* very suitable, it's rather small, but with as I said some interesting features, and totally discreet, complete privacy.'

Eterson relaxed visibly. 'Call me Simon,' he said and leaned back, 'please call me Simon.'

That the *My Thai* was in one of the seedier districts of downtown Bangkok, you could certainly see from the streets along which they drove. Crowded pavements, flashy neon signs, and hoards of people endlessly crossing the roads. Hundreds of Japanese, on their famous sex tours, could be seen making their way into the massage parlours. Girls in various stages of undress were sitting in the windows, row on row of them, each with a tag round her neck, waiting to be called. Mike could see Eterson next to him almost slobbering, wide-eyed with pleasure. Actually he didn't really have to go this way but he always did, it got them going a bit.

They came to a cross roads and Mike turned left, and into one of the narrow side roads. After a mile they turned through iron gates into the wide courtyard of a villa. It was dimly lit, but Eterson could see that a number of cars were already parked near the stone staircase which led up into the building. A small sign could just be made out, and by it stood a well-dressed young Thai with a commissionaire's hat just a size too big for him. They parked and Mike turned to his passenger. 'This is it, sir, one of the most private places around; good food too.' Eterson watched as he locked the car door and gave the keys and a note to the young man. Obviously the place was well-run, and they knew Mike, the two of them were having a whispered conversation. Eterson was sure that money was passing hands again. This James, he thought, may be a youngster, but he certainly knows his way around. The attendant left them and went to a phone at the foot of the stairs. As he spoke into it, Mike put his arm around Eterson. 'Off we go, sir,' he said, 'service assured, let's go in and enjoy ourselves.'

'Mike,' said Eterson, wiping sauce from his mouth with a large white napkin, 'that was bloody marvellous.' They had been taken by the head waiter into the club and shown to a table on a balcony which looked down onto a stage. The club wasn't big, it sat about fifty, but the fifty were arranged at tables seating six or eight, around the balcony. Each table though had a good view of the small stage and was completely private. Thick red curtains at the sides and back. The chairs were small double couches in the same material. Candles flickered on the table and it was cosy and private, just as Mike had promised. The food had been excellent. A ricetable of different Thai specialities, served quickly and efficiently by the young waiters. They were now washing it down with the local beer. Eterson leaned back. 'Just wait,' said Mike, 'cabaret starts any time now.' Almost on cue, the single light above the stage went out, there was a hush, and a spotlight stabbed through the darkness.

A low chanting, soothing music started up and Eterson leaned forward. He was not disappointed. Up until now he hadn't seen a single woman in the place, but his eyes widened as two beautiful young girls moved onto the stage dancing in time to the music. They couldn't be more than sixteen he thought. Their slow, sensuous movements were designed to entrance. The tempo increased, and the girls began to touch each other, slowly at first, teasing, and then more intimately. Eterson swallowed hard but his eyes didn't leave them. They were now undressing each other, kissing and caressing each other's bodies, fingers, lips and limbs exploring every possible place.

Mike sat back, bored. He'd seen this show any number of times and he was jaded by it. He took his pleasure by looking at the face of his guest; he waited until Eterson's tongue licked his lips and then looked down. Yes, the two were well into their act. He sat back and poured himself another beer. Plenty of time he thought, and glanced at his watch, let the tension mount.

The girls were now joined by an older woman. Eterson couldn't believe his eyes, she was dressed in leather from head to toe, and carrying a whip. He was beside himself and then he felt Mike's hand on his shoulder. 'I'll leave you now sir,' he said, 'but you won't be alone. Please enjoy yourself. The car will take you home when you're ready.'

Eterson was a bit taken aback, but as Mike drew the curtains to go, two girls came through the curtains, pulled the table back out of the way and in a second were sitting next to him. He felt a hand reaching gently between his thighs, and he stiffened under the caress. The other girl whispered. 'Stay,' she said, 'we will make you happy' and they giggled. He grinned at them both, damn good show, he thought.

Eterson was collected the next morning from the hotel at ten-thirty. Mike was courteous and polite. He'd been a bit nervous first thing this morning, after he realised what he'd done, but when he thought of the two girls and their naked bodies in the candle-light he smiled to himself. Now he was feeling quite proud. You old dog he thought, not bad for your age, eh? The bill had been a bit steep, but you only live once. Wait until he got back to the UK and saw his pals at the club. Have to be a bit careful about telling them, but they'd know all right. Good job this boy James was the soul of discretion. Jolly good show. Now of course he'd got to visit this boring office. Still, the piper had to be paid, and would he have a story for his pals when he got back.

The office was boring. Old Worthington was putting on his usual dog-and-pony show. He'd introduced all the staff, gone through all the figures, and then pointedly asked Eterson if he'd enjoyed his evening. Mike was there all the time in the background, deferential as ever. There was a bit of a strained atmosphere, everyone knowing just how unnecessary the visit was. Still, Eterson could cope with that, after all he thought, I'm the Senior Manager. These people are only here to serve the greater company good, and that included looking after him.

Mike sensed it as well, they all acted this way, humble at first when they arrived, then pally in the evening, then nervous and unsure in the morning. Then they'd start to assert themselves in the office and before long, they'd get resentful. He was waiting now, like the office junior he was, outside Worthington's office and he could hear the clink of glasses. Bloody typical, he thought. I do all the running around, I do all the entertaining, and bloody Worthington will get all the credit in the report Eterson would make and send to Head Office. He was bored, pissed off, he didn't want to spend the next few years pimping for senior bloody management. Still, he'd learned a trick or two, after the first couple of times.

He took out of his pocket an envelope, opened it up and grinned at the contents. This was another lot, to add to the collection. Screw Worthington. When he went back to the UK on leave next month, he'd go and see the Head of Personnel, Blenkin. He'd been one of his visitors here, just like Eterson. They were all going to help him on his way. After all, he'd got photos of all of them. He looked again, yes it was really quite good, the way the naked bodies stood out against the thick red curtains in the candle-light.

────Running For Cover────

VICTOR WILLIAMS was an actuary. You know what they say about actuaries. They tend to be refugees from the accounting profession which they left because they found it too exciting. Victor was such a person.

Quiet, unassuming and meticulous in appearance, attitude and application . . . Give Victor a client's dusty ledger full of scribbled entries and he would be lost for weeks in an intrinsic search for the truth. Figures were the truth for Victor. Facts were facts, order was order, laws were there to be obeyed. Stability was his hallmark, regularity his byword.

A short report would be issued after his analysis was complete. It would be full of formulae, statistical trends and conclusions. These tomes would be passed on and utilised by lesser mortals in the insurance companies which were his organisations' main clients. His particular speciality was the company audit. He positively enjoyed the role of inquisitor and if there was any evidence of fraud, then Victor was on to it. There was many a company director enjoying Her Majesty's hospitality who owed his downfall to Victor's eagle eye. A paragon of company and personal virtue.

His profession and values didn't mean that Victor was in any way a boring character. Far from it. He was married to his former secretary, who understood him and his ways, and they had two children. Due to the high salaries paid to members of his profession, he had a large comfortably furnished country house in Redhill just outside London and his children went to the best local private schools. His wife indulged her passions for tennis and horseriding on an almost daily basis and Victor collected and drank vintage wines. He also never went without his early morning jog. He left home every morning, summer, winter, rain or shine, light or dark, at 6.30 am and ran for about thirty minutes out into the fields and hills surrounding his house. His morning exercise and communion with nature were very important to him. A strong sense of correctness ran through

Victor's life, values and daily routine.

It came as somewhat of a shock therefore to an individual who liked this orderly existence, and hated change, to be asked by the Managing Partner of his company to undertake an overseas audit. He was horrified by the prospect! One week in Minneapolis to go through the books of a local insurance company that one of his UK clients was thinking of purchasing. He had thought of refusing, so upset had he been, but one look at the Managing Partner's face had told him that this was not a request, but an order. Victor had nodded in compliance as was in his character.

His wife had at first been excited when he told her, but when she saw his reaction, had lapsed into commiserating understanding. Apart from a two week package tour each year to a cocooned existence in a hotel resort in Southern Spain, Victor had never really been abroad. As he packed for the trip he had felt desolate and only cheered up when his wife suggested he take his running gear with him as he might get a chance for a jog. He had demurred at first but then warmed to the idea. It gave him a sense of security to think that part of his routine would go with him into the strange environment. He resolved that this part of his day would remain unchanged. His farewells to the family had been like a wake and he almost willed the taxi to be late for the airport. It was not to be.

Cushioned, however, by the comfort of his first class seat, direct flight and some very good claret, served to him by the attentive stewardesses, he began to relax. He felt better in the cosy cabin and looked forward to reading his book.

Poor Victor, he hadn't reckoned without that curse of every international traveller's life, the busybody. His next door neighbour on the plane was such a person. The busybodies of the world seem to believe that everyone is interested in their lives in the most minute detail and their opinions on everything. The gentleman next to Victor fastened on his victim like a vampire would on the neck of a young girl. He quickly discovered that Victor had not been to the States before and saw it as his holy duty to educate him.

At the end of that nine hour flight when his tormenter had bade farewell, Victor's head held a hellish version of America as a place where civilization had broken down. Muggers roamed the streets in broad daylight and murders and robberies were commonplace. Orderly men can cope with no other view of the world except their own and Victor's world was shaken by the revelations of his fellow traveller.

Getting out of the plane and through immigration and customs was a nightmare and he was so nervous that he hardly spoke to the local taxi driver, a friendly enough soul, right up until he paid him off at the hotel. He rushed into the lobby, booked in and only started to feel secure when he got into his room. Thank God, he thought, that all hotels were the same across the world. He was exhausted by his ordeal and staggered to bed.

He woke up early in the morning and, pulling the curtains, looked out of the window. Opposite he saw to his delight a magnificent panorama. A huge vista of parkland stretched as far as the eye could see. It was almost like the view from his own home over the North Downs. He remembered his promise to himself. He glanced at his watch, he had plenty of time for his jog.

Why should he, he thought, as he pulled on his tracksuit, change his routine just because he was three or four thousand miles from home. In fact he could see as he tied his laces in front of the window that there were already a number of early morning runners and cyclists dotted around the park. Yesterday's troubled thoughts washed away by his sleep, did not even surface, Victor was transported to normality.

He trotted out of the hotel and gingerly picked his way across the freeway busy with traffic. A careful man as always, he stopped at the park gates and chose the most deserted path which reached out across the meadow and went into the trees about half a mile away. He set off on his usual loping pace breathing deeply.

He wasn't in a foreign country. In his mind's eye he was back at home moving across the fields on the track through the woods that he always followed. He kept on going and the path pushed into the trees. A dark silent world, with only the birds and his laboured but regular breathing, kept him company. He was so preoccupied that he almost fell into the water which suddenly appeared around a sharp turn.

It was a magnificent lake and Victor turned swiftly to the left and began running along its shoreline. There was no one else around except a figure running like him along the far shore. Victor looked ahead of him and kept on going running alongside

the lake as the path took him into the trees away from the water for two or three hundred yards and then back again. He was lost in his normal morning ritual, comfortable and secure. It was on one of the curves that it happened!

The other jogger was running around a corner going full pelt, and Victor was running around a corner going full pelt. The trees were thick at that point and neither of them saw the other.

There was a collision. The runner fell and his arms went around Victor's waist pulling his clothing. There was a muttered 'sorry' from both of them as they reeled and stumbled, and then the jogger was on his feet and off running. Victor stopped slightly out of breath and then gathering himself ran on. Something wasn't right? He gasped, and his hand went to his back pocket, his wallet had gone! He was stunned, that hadn't been an accident. He felt again and shuddered. Fear flooded into his brain. The conversations of the night before came flooding back. He'd been mugged.

He cursed, what a fool. Running in the woods early in the morning, no wonder all the rest of the early morning exercisers had kept to the safety of the outer ring of the park. An anger welled up in him, he turned about in a blind fury, his face flushed, and ran after his assailant. Victor's sense of order had been violated and emotions he scarcely knew drove him to pursuit.

His gaze narrowed and his legs pushed forward with a pent up furious energy. Within a few minutes he saw in a break in the path the attacker about three hundred yards in front. He quickened his pace and within five minutes he was just a hundred yards behind. He shouted and saw the man turn and glance nervously over his shoulder at him. The man also increased his pace but not to be outdone, Victor sped on. He was catching up fast.

He was only ten yards behind when he started to scream at the top of his voice, 'Drop the wallet, drop the wallet.'

The jogger didn't even turn; his hand went to his back pocket and he threw the wallet over his head in an arc. It dropped straight in front of Victor who leant down, grabbed it quickly and charged on still screaming. A devil possessed him. The jogger in front was panicked and sped off. Victor, bent on revenge, ran after him, but now he had recovered his possession began to tire, and the hunted drew ahead of the hunter. Victor realised he'd lost him. The chase was over, but although he was exhausted he kept on going. His one thought now was to get out of the park and back to the safety of his room. The sooner he could get there the better. He was shaking with the shock of it, but a quiet satisfaction with its outcome kept his legs moving. The jogger was nowhere to be seen.

Victor stumbled to the hotel, grabbed his key from the desk clerk and jumped into the lift, pushing the buttons with pent up fury. What an idiot he had been! He twisted the key in the lock and shouldered his way into the sanctuary of the room. Panting heavily he glanced in the mirror. He saw in its reflection his pained face, twisted with exertion and fear. He looked down and up again. Now there was something else reflected, sheer horror. He had not been the victim after all. He looked down unbelievingly. The papers that he'd left on the table the night before. Nestled among them was his wallet, just where he'd put it before he'd gone to bed.

The Return
——Of Captain Cook——

I HADN'T GONE to Hawaii, but William had. Along with all the other Senior Managers, he'd got his invitation to the world-wide bi-annual shindig two months ago. And, like all the other Senior Managers, he'd never missed an opportunity to ask me if I was going. When I had answered in the negative, he had seemed surprised.

I had been a bit put out to tell the truth and wondered who I'd upset recently on the board. Let no-one convince you that working for a company is anything more than joining a tribe. You give your loyalty and skills and hard labour, they give you a share in the proceeds. As long, that is, as you observe the pecking order. William and other members of the European tribunal delegation went to the pow-wow in Honolulu. I went back to my desk to man the fort.

I didn't really mind because William was an old schoolfriend and he promised to tell me about it at the Club when he got back. We lunched there regularly, part of the ritual which we'd observed for over ten years, although there had been gaps when I'd been assigned to Belgium for three years and when he'd done a tour in Italy. We much enjoyed our monthly get-togethers. Lunch and reminiscing about our old schooldays was what kept us both sane in the hurly-burly world of high international finance to which we belonged.

It was therefore with great expectations that I now sat in the dining room on the first floor of the Club in Charlotte Street and nursed my dry sherry at our regular table, waiting for William to arrive and to hear how he'd got on. Margaret, one of the Club's servants, came over with the menu. She was Irish, from Kilkenny, and had been around for donkey's years, long before I became a member. She raised her eyebrows towards the empty seat.

'Will you be wanting the menu yet?' she said. 'Or shall I wait for Mr William to arrive?'

'Oh, leave them on the table, Margaret,' I replied. 'I am sure he will be here soon.'

'I am sure he will, soir,' she snorted. 'And no doubt he'll be telling you more about his adventures.'

I smiled. Margaret didn't approve of William, many people didn't. You see, he was a bachelor and had a bit of a reputation as a womanizer. Most of the members of our Club were married and staid and that was the way they liked it. William, on the other hand, hadn't ever got anywhere near marriage. Hit 'em and run, was his motto, and judging from the rumours that I'd heard about his father, that had run in the family. William never talked about his family. His father was a bit of a mystery but a number of the Club's older members had known him by reputation, whatever that had been.

Any reference to this parent always brought grins and sly winks. Undoubtedly the members accepted William because they had known and liked his father and all I could surmise was that he had been a bit of a rake as well. William, as far as I was concerned, was an old school chum, damned good company, and of course, he'd been in the Guards.

William came into the dining room, looking as dapper as ever. Six foot one, double-breasted blue striped suit from Saville Row, immaculate as ever. Bronzed face, no doubt from the Hawaiian sun, I ruefully thought, and his black, brilliantined hair swathed back from his high forehead. He didn't have, I noticed, much of a bounce in his step and alarm bells rang momentarily in my mind. He wasn't even smiling, which was most unusual for William. He grunted and sat down. 'I wonder whats up?' I thought. Not the William we all knew and loved. He could see the consternation on my face.

'Order first,' he said. 'Then I'll tell you all about it.'

He ordered. William acknowledged Margaret as she handed him his dry sherry and he started to smile and talk. That was better, I thought. More like the William I knew.

'I travelled with Peter from Los Angeles. It was quite amusing really.' Ah ha! I thought, a tale. I waited expectantly. 'The airline we'd booked on was on strike and the only flight we could get was a honeymoon special. We didn't realise it until we'd got into the first class cabin, and then we saw the stewardess give us a quizzical glance as she showed us to our seats. The only male couple in the cabin, all the rest were starry-eyed youngsters of the opposite sex. Well, you know me and you know Peter. It was a heaven-sent opportunity, old man. When they served the champagne, would you believe it, in warm plastic glasses, with a cherry!'

I shuddered at that point and I could see several of the members at the next table who couldn't help overhearing the conversation, grimace. Warm champagne, cherries, plastic glasses. Heresy!

'Well,' continued William. 'I turned to Peter, winked at him, and we toasted each other loudly, "To our future happiness darling". And we blew each other kisses. We kept the whole charade up right the way through the journey.' I laughed loudly picturing the scene, the next table could scarcely contain themselves as well.

William continued as the soup arrived.

'Anyway, when we came in to land there was the most beautiful sunset and the most delightful wahines to meet us with those flower garlands they put around every tourist. Well, anyway, those from first class.'

William and I ate our soup in silence, manners had to be preserved but I could see as we finished that a number of the members had been listening intently, William's reputation as a bit of a lad was well known and you could see that everyone was interested in how the story would develop. He continued.

'You should have seen the lobby at the Wakiki Beach Hotel. It was like one of those horrible new shopping centres. At least 200 yards long and 50 yards wide.'

'Get on with the story, man,' I interrupted, as the entrée arrived. William grinned. The next table I could see were still attentive and William knew it.

'Well, the conference was the usual thing,' he went on. 'There must have been 300 of us, all listening to the speeches and razzamatazz. Do you know this year they even had a company song? Bloody well went down a treat, I tell you. Americans loved it, Europeans hated it. South Americans tolerated it and well, our Aussie cousins were too drunk to notice anything.' I smiled appreciatively, it confirmed all my old colonial prejudices.

'Anyway, the big event was on the last evening and I must give the Yanks their due. They'd laid out tables in the gardens,

beautiful weather, balmy night, twinkling stars, crashing surf in the background and the marvellous perfume of the wonderful oleander flowers. Every table was surrounded with flaming candles, quite a show, I tell you. Oh, I forgot, they'd dished out Hawaiian shirts for everyone to wear. Mine was all flowers and silk. Make a damn good pyjama jacket.'

We finished the entrée. William continued, 'The food was delightful, the tropical fruit marvellous, probably flown in from California, though. Plenty of beer on the table but the wine, well, quite disgusting really.' William gratefully helped himself to more of the Club claret, as the roast arrived.

'Then, we thought, that was it. Good meal, good company, but old Whatsisname, the President, hadn't finished. Suddenly the lights went out and there in the background by the palm trees was a floodlit stage with the most amazing spectacle.'

William paused, well aware of the importance of timing to his audience. I glanced around, half the Club seemed to be listening. 'There were about forty wahines, gorgeous young, brown-skinned girls, grass skirts, the lot, dancing in the most sensuous way, just to the beat of the drums in the background. I tell you, it fairly took a fellow's breath away. The whole conference were taken completely by surprise. It was the most amazing scene.'

William broke off and smiled at Margaret, who had descended to clear away the main course. I, (and I could see over William's shoulder, all the other tables nearby) were absolutely riveted and resented the interruption. I could almost see the palm trees and feel the warm breeze in the dining room.

'Well, to continue,' William said, attacking the spotted dick and custard which Margaret had brought us.

'Well, these wahines – lovely, they were,' he repeated, 'were weaving their way between the tables. Their bodies were moving in time to the music and every male eye was following every sensuous move their glorious tanned stomachs were making. The leading girl had obviously been briefed to waltz around our table because of the big cheese sitting at it, and she ended up dancing right in front of us. I tell you, old man, I have never seen anything like it. She was about five foot three tall, long, dark hair down to her waist, glistening skin, a grass skirt that swished open with the beat to reveal the most heavenly pair of legs I have ever seen.'

I could see over William's shoulder that the members were practically hanging on every word he said, and drooling at the mouth at the thought of it. I myself was quite carried away, our dining room seemed to be part of the Hawaiian landscape, a terrace with waving palm trees, starlit skies and rhythmic beats pulsing around. I savoured the moment and waited on William's words. William had gone quiet. His eyes had a funny look to them.

'What happened?' I said, in expectation. William grinned.

'Well,' he said in a whisper, 'never seen such a pretty filly in all my life. I was just bowled over.'

The members around us could be seen to take in their breaths.

'Well,' I said. 'What happened next?'

'Well, that's the rub' William continued. 'What could I say? I had to say something because I had to see her again but I couldn't really interrupt the performance, particularly in front of the President.'

'Then,' William said, and he leant forward with an earnest look on his face, 'I hit on it. Quite frankly, it went down quite well. I looked her straight in the eyes and raised my voice above the music. She looked at me. I caught her attention and then, at the top of my voice, I shouted out "Oh, to be Captain Cook!" '

I, and the whole of the Club dining room burst out laughing. The air of tension and expectation went. I smiled at William. 'William,' I said, and the whole Club thought, 'Winding us up again!'

I was so amused that I didn't really notice William's face, he hadn't taken the Club's reaction at all well. He'd looked in amazement at me and turned to see the others laughing. He'd then gone very quiet and finished his plate in silence. Shortly after he made his excuses and left. I was left to grin and relate everything that I had heard and the others hadn't, at the bar, to half the Club afterwards.

'Just like his father,' one of the older members said. 'He could tell a tale or two.'

William sent his excuses a month later about not being able to get together for lunch and indeed, the month after that. I didn't worry very much but one evening at home with my wife, reading *The Times*, I saw an announcement. I started and turned to my wife and pointed it out. In the engagements columns was an announcement about William. He was marrying a girl with a very strange name. Was it the girl who he had fallen for in Hawaii? I told my wife the story of William's escapade.

'Well, well' said my wife. 'Fancy old William doing that, just like his father.'

'Oh really,' I said, 'just like his father?'

'Oh yes,' she said, 'great scandal daddy said, met, went off and lived with some native woman in India after the war. Family never forgave him, left William's mother all alone with the boy.'

'Dear, oh, dear,' I said. My wife nodded and I tried to think of who else from my old school days I could lunch with at the Club once a month.

The Head-dress

WE WERE COMING in to land at Riyadh. It was my second trip to Saudi; the first being three months ago at Jeddah. The flight and approach had been over desert – hundreds of miles of it. Low, flat dunes, curving plains of greyish-yellow sand stretching continuously for as far as the eye could see. The plane shuddered to a stop. I could see the heat haze shimmering off the wings and the tarmac. Jeddah had been hospitable all those months ago but Riyadh was not inviting on first impression. First impressions however, could be wrong as I'd learnt. I scurried out, following a mixed bag of European businessmen, in the minority, and Arabs, in the majority.

I recalled my previous experiences as the bus bounced across to the arrivals hall. How wrong I'd been to think of the country as backward and unsophisticated.

For my sins, I represented an international company that like many others, had been seduced by the prospects of doing business in oil-rich Saudi. My chief executive back home in the UK had given me the dubious privilege of following his hunches through. He had some vague connections with one of the many Saudi princes and felt that this was a heaven sent opportunity to develop our business in the country. The first stage was to see whether we could expand our two small agency offices in Jeddah and Riyadh into a more substantial network. Within a few days of his decision, I got my visa and with a great deal of trepidation had flown into the old Red Sea trading port. I had then been pleasantly surprised.

The first surprise had been my host, our agent in Jeddah, whose office had been situated in the old part of town, above one of the many shops in the souk or local bazaar. Abdullah was a wily, old, Saudi trader, whose father (or so he told me), had followed Lawrence's army in Palestine, selling pots, pans and anything else they needed. With the money he'd made, he'd then set up shop in Jeddah and proceeded to have two wives, six sons and build a business. He had died many years ago but Abdullah,

43

the eldest son, talked fondly of his father and made me feel immediately at home and one of his extended family.

The second surprise was to find that the courtesy, good manners and hospitality lavished on me was not just by Abdullah himself. It was a deeply engraved part of every Saudi's psyche and everyone that Abdullah introduced me to displayed the same civilized charm.

It went back to the days in the desert, it was explained to me. If you'd been sitting in your tent with just the same old tribe to keep you company day after day and night after night and then happened on a stranger, well, you took him in and looked after him for his company. It was more your pleasure than his, as a welcome diversion for three or four days. The rituals were precise and strictly followed. The reward, an opportunity to learn some news, share a few stories and enjoy a feast. Give a Saudi a cup of coffee or mint tea and some good companions and he'd talk and talk, and keep you amused all day and night!

That had certainly been Abdullah. I'd really enjoyed his company until one night. We'd been sitting around in his flat talking away, when suddenly the lights had gone out. Abdullah, who up until then had been mine host, joviality itself, suddenly got very scared. He'd leapt up, got a torch and immediately rushed over and bolted the door. He was very agitated shouting commands which I quickly obeyed, rushing up the stairs and scrambling out to a low, flat terrace. I could now see under the light of the stars that the whole city seemed to be blacked out. We could hear other people on their close-by roofs and there was some frantic shouting between houses. We'd only been there a few minutes and I wondered what on earth was going on, when suddenly the lights came back on. I sighed with relief, but Abdullah hadn't. He was biting his nails and looking very pale. He rushed downstairs and I made my way gingerly after him. He was already on the phone and was gabbling on to someone at the other end. When he put the receiver down he told me that there was trouble and that I'd better get back to the hotel as quickly as possible. I was bemused but also scared myself.

I'd found out about the trouble later from the hotel manager, who came solemnly up to me at breakfast the next morning.

'My advice to you,' he had said, 'is to leave and go home!' He wouldn't tell me why in front of the other customers, but told me to see him in his office later. I could certainly tell something was up because, amongst all the guests were a large number of locals and they were distinctly nervous, talking hurriedly to themselves with many glances over their shoulders and all of them fingering their worry beads.

'What's the problem?' I enquired of the manager, when I went to his office later. He got up and closed the door.

'I am told,' he said, 'that a group of religious fanatics have taken over the Grand Mosque at Mecca. They are led by a Mahdi.' He saw my quizzical expression. 'A Holy One, a Messiah to you Christians. Apparently this man and his followers entered the mosque and have declared that they are the true descendants of Mohammed and that the Mullahs and the Government should recognize them as such.' I looked at him in amazement, open mouthed.

'Well, what are the Government doing about it?' I'd enquired. He was deadly serious.

'The King has given permission for troops to enter the Holy Shrine and remove these heretics.' I began to understand what had happened the night before at Abdullah's. It obviously had a connection with the black-out and my friend's reaction. I'd thanked the manager and confirmed that in the circumstances I'd better get out quickly. I left a note for Abdullah thanking him for his hospitality. I packed, paid and was off to the airport within an hour.

A lot of other people seemed to have the same idea as me and not just visiting businessmen. There were crowds of people at the airport, all with the same worried expressions as Abdullah had had the night before, and all of them fingering their beads. I'd used my good offices with British Airways to get on a plane to Athens and, by the end of the day, I had winged my way out of the town. It was a relief to be off.

When I got back to London, I had to put up with a great deal of leg-pulling about my adventure. The papers were full of the story, and I followed the action closely. The Mosque had been, besieged for about a week by the army before all the heretics had been killed or captured. The Mahdi had been amongst them. Gradually the whole thing quietened down and three months almost to the day, my chief executive decided that the country was stable and having received assurances from Abdullah that everything had settled down, bade me make a trip to see the agent in Riyadh.

So here I was back amongst the Arabs. Everything looked peaceful enough at Riyadh airport and I grabbed a taxi after, to my surprise, getting through immigration very quickly.

'A lot of building work going on,' I said to my driver as we bounced over the rough roads on the outskirts of town. His reply was immediate.

'Praise be to God,' he said. 'Once we were a poor country but now, blessings be upon Him, we are rich. It is a reward for keeping the Holy places. Now we are seeing the benefits. It is just.' He didn't speak again for ten more bouncing minutes.

'Your hotel is over there,' he shouted. I stared into the distance. We hadn't come anywhere near a town, we'd just been driving around on these dusty old roads. But I could see where the driver was pointing and it was just another gigantic building site.

'There must be some mistake,' I said.

'No, no! No mistake,' he said. 'Hotel is built on the site of the new airport.' We looked at each other. I was perplexed. What new airport? I couldn't see anything for miles around, just desert. We drew into the supposed hotel complex and I was somewhat reassured to find that it was obviously not a building site itself, although construction was going on all around it.

'Why is it,' I thought, 'that every hotel across the world looks the same?' I drew my luggage out of the boot and stood in the forecourt looking into the middle of nowhere. 'Home sweet home!' I said aloud and paid off the driver, who thanked me profusely with many blessings upon me. They seemed, I mused, to be more religious here than in Jeddah, but very courteous.

I trundled into the air-conditioned lobby and had a pleasant surprise. A civilized interior greeted me.

The floor was marbled, as was the reception counter and the lobby opened up into a vast, cavernous hall. In the middle, with pillars standing all around it was a huge fountain, trickling water. A fountain was a feature that all Arabs liked to have and most houses were laid out that way. From the outside, what seemed to be squat, square fortresses were, in fact, magnificent palaces for whole extended families who could live in four or more separate flats, all surrounding a cool, shaded courtyard with flowing fountains in the middle. It was restful, and an obvious retreat from the harsh desert environment that they were used to.

Around my hotel lobby fountain were scattered rugs of every hue and shape, and on these were placed low tables. Groups of Arab businessmen in their red head-dresses and white robes were sitting, chatting and smoking and forever pouring cups of mint tea or coffee from the magnificent silver and gold pots which seemed a permanent feature on each table. The domed roof was crowned with a huge circular hoop and from this swathes of tent-like material stretched down to the pillars surrounding the central area.

'Fairly takes your breath away,' I said to the smiling desk clerk as I signed the register. No one looked up as I followed the Filipino porter, weaving our way around the sitting and gossiping groups, to the lift. I tipped my man as he dumped the bags in my room and asked him how far I was from Riyadh itself.

'About twenty minutes,' he replied, 'on the new road. Just go down to the reception and they'll get you a taxi.' I thanked him, and decided to crash out for the night. I was feeling comfortable and cosseted.

Breakfast was routine consisting of the standard fare served all over the world, and I plotted my day as I munched through the croissants, orange juice and coffee. I'd found out in Jeddah that my Westerner's idea of time and diary organization meant very little in this part of the world. It seems that values are reversed. I remembered the experience I'd had in the Government office in Jeddah three months ago, waiting to see the contact that had been recommended to me by Abdullah.

'An important man,' Abdullah had said, 'the Sheik, and very difficult to see, but here is a letter of introduction for you.' I'd duly turned up at the Government office where the Sheik was based and had been surprised to see that it was completely surrounded by a large perimeter wall with just a double wooden gate entrance. It seemed to be something out of the French Foreign Legion. The taxi circled this monstrosity and left me. I stood looking at the huge gate, wondering how on earth I was going to get in? I'd eventually examined it, and seen a brass knocker which I ended up banging, feeling utterly foolish. The door had opened to reveal a small man in military uniform, who eyed me very slowly up and down. Eventually he took the letter of introduction, which I held out to him. He then closed the door without saying a word; reappearing some fifteen minutes later, when I was just about to give up hope of ever seeing him again, with a similarly dressed individual, but this man had a stripe on his arm. He also read the letter, glanced at me, and then the two of them had gone inside the door.

I had stood sweating under the sun, bemused by the whole process, when the door bolts could be heard swinging back and there in front of me, with two guards, stood a jeep with what was clearly an officer holding my letter and beckoning me into the vehicle. This process of identification and ratification from the bottom rank to the higher rank continued. Then after a short drive to the Ministry proper, I was shown around the back to what looked like a tradesman's entrance, where yet other guards (this time armed, I noticed) relieved my driver, read the letter and motioned me to sit on a bench in what seemed to be the guards' room. I was not amused.

I'd sat like that for an hour, figuring out what I should do next. I had just decided to try and find out what was going on, when a familiar figure emerged from the doorway leading into the depths of the Ministry. It was Abdullah, dressed in a ceremonial garb I'd never seen before. He greeted me as if nothing had happened and before I had time to question him, had shown me into a large ante-room adjoining the guards' quarters.

It was like going into a market. Around the room were seated at the most simple desks a number of splendidly robed Ministry officials and in front of each one of them was a large crowd of similarly dressed Arabs, all shouting and gesticulating and waving papers.

It apparently was Petitioners' Day, Abdullah explained. Any citizen who had a legitimate grievance had to draw up a petition and present it to the relevant Ministry. If the petition was accepted, then the official who took it was honour bound to deal with it. It was even explained to me that the King was duty bound to receive his citizens every month and deal with them and their grievances, in the same way. I'd shaken my head at the scene in disbelief initially, but then reflected on how democratic it all was.

Abdullah showed me to another bench outside a door at the far end of the room and I sat like a dummy, looking at the milling people in front of me. Just before he'd left, Abdullah had explained to me that the longer I waited the more important a person I was perceived to be! This was the Arab way of doing things and was, as you can imagine, some comfort to me, as two hours passed slowly. It was only when I again was despairing of anything happening, that I was suddenly confronted with a servant, offering me coffee. I had learned that this was the Saudi introduction. If you had three thimbleful cups of bitter, black Saudi coffee, not one cup less, not one cup more, and when you had had the third cup, you turned it over to indicate that your needs had been satisfied, it completed a ritual which meant that your host was then ready to talk business.

The servant had stood impassively by while I went through the coffee drinking and nodded approvingly at my good manners, he had then shown me into the elusive Sheik's room. Again, I had sat down and nobody took any notice of me for a further quarter of an hour. Finally, the Sheik had turned to me and in impeccable English that absolutely floored me had said:

'I see you live in Brighton. What do you think of Roedean as a school?'

I laughed to myself, recalling him. I'd spent the rest of my so-called interview discussing the pros and cons of an English public school education for the Sheik's daughter.

Mint tea, another Saudi courtesy and custom had been drunk continuously and from time to time, when I had tried to introduce the real purpose of my visit, this immensely courteous and hospitable person politely declined to discuss it, preferring to question me on the school's situation. It was a big decision for the Sheik, as he had two wives and six daughters. Under Islamic law, he explained to me, he was duty bound to provide both his wives' families with an exactly similar standard of living. A decision, therefore, to send his eldest daughter to one school in one country would set a precedent to be followed by all the others. Again I thought how sensible that was, something we in the West could learn from. It was only when a bell rang in the corridor that he got up, thanked me warmly and motioned me to go.

'It is time,' he said, 'for prayers and we do not like infidels to share or see our devotions. You will have no problem in expanding your business. Get Abdullah to confirm your plans and I will get the necessary permission.'

I was amazed. That was it! More surprised perhaps, by being called an infidel than the way of doing business.

That was the main reason I'd now returned. I'd agreed to

49

plans with Abdullah and needed to wrap up the formalities with our local representative in Riyadh. The agent had a small office in the Intercontinental Hotel in the centre of the city and I was seeing him tomorrow after I'd got well over any jet lag. It is never a good idea to do business soon after you arrive after a long flight and journey.

Breakfast was now being cleared away. It was already ten o'clock. I'd got the whole day to relax and thought that I'd go into town and the local bazaar and do some shopping.

Given my experiences in Jeddah on timekeeping, and appointments, it would certainly pay to make a preliminary call to the agent, just to stop over at the Intercontinental and leave my card so as to make sure of seeing him on the morrow.

The heat and light outside the hotel really hit me after the air-conditioned comfort within. I was glad I was dressed comfortably, slacks, shirt and sunglasses. The sun was a great red ball sitting in a clear, blue sky, beating down mercilessly, which was another good reason for taking it easy on my first day. Acclimatization is essential to sound thinking. I was sweating within minutes, the taxis were in a row about fifty yards from the entrance. I soon saw why they were fifty yards away. They were parked in the shade of the building and probably worked their way around as the sun shifted the shadow. One drew up – an air-conditioned Mercedes, and I told the driver in pigeon English, because I only knew one word of Arabic, where to go. 'Insh'Allah' was the word I knew – 'as God wills it.' The driver nodded and replied with the same one word.

It was comfortable, sitting in the cool interior and this time we had a chance to look at the scenery. Well, you could call it scenery if you liked. It was really just a new town being carved out of the desert. It did, I noticed, have some interesting contradictions. The motorways and roads were built American-style – great broad, five-laned in each direction, highways. The city streets on the other hand, because they were so wide, looked as if they'd been laid out by Frenchmen as boulevards. The buildings which lined either side of these streets seemed to have been designed by either modernist German architects or English country builders. They were either blocks of steel, glass and concrete or copies of Regency town or Oxford manorial splendours.

The Intercontinental, however, was an Intercontinental, just the same as any others and instantly recognizable to the

50

travelling businessman. I drew up outside and a gold-braided, peak capped commissionaire opened the door. I explained what I'd come for and that I wouldn't be long and he gave the driver directions to the parking area. I was then ushered through the portals and pointed across the nondescript lobby to a corridor where it was indicated our agent had his offices.

As I said, I'd only intended to drop my card in but it was not to be. Courtesy and custom wouldn't allow it. The small office housed two Pakistani clerks huddled over telex machines and, as the proprietor was out and expecting me on the morrow, they insisted I had coffee with them. They said that dire punishment would befall them if their boss found out that I had visited and not been formally welcomed by them. I explained that I wanted to visit the souk but they waived aside my protests with cries of 'Plenty of time. Sit and have coffee.'

It was already nearly eleven but I sat and reconciled myself good-naturedly to the ritual. The coffee was a long time coming and although I chatted pleasantly enough about working in Saudi, and cricket, which they both missed enormously, it was clear that I was going to miss the souk which shut, as I knew, dead on the dot of twelve for prayers. Consequently, it was twenty five to twelve before I got away, obligations having been fulfilled on both sides satisfactorily.

'Bloody hell!' I exclaimed, looking at my watch. 'Have I got time to get some shopping in?'

'Sod it,' I thought, 'I might as well go and have a look at the souk, as I might not get another chance. There might by something open, so I could pick up the souvenir I needed.'

It was no good telling the driver to hurry. He'd already waited patiently for me. So, I just shouted 'souk' at him and pointed madly at my watch. He shrugged his shoulders, said the obligatory 'Insh'Allah' and drove off at the same pace as we'd come to the hotel.

It didn't, however, take us long to get there, about ten minutes. My driver drew up in a crowded market square and gesticulated across to it. He indicated he would wait at the same spot and I rushed out with ten minutes to spare to closing time.

The Souk was a riot of colours, people and noise and I plunged joyously into it. I was soon grabbed by an English speaking stallholder and dragged back to his shop. He found out what I wanted and fussed around me, fitting the red and white

chequered cloth on my head and fixing it with the black headband that kept it in place. The head-dress had no special significance, it was just a fashion which seemed to be a Saudi trademark. Every few seconds the trader would stand back to admire his handiwork, beaming broadly at me and pointing with pride to my cracked image in his cracked mirror. I counted out the price we'd haggled over. Leaving him still grinning broadly, I'd probably paid too much, I made my way out of the building joining the throng with my new possession still on. I'd got it at last. A quick walkabout, then back to the hotel.

There was a rush; nearly midday. I saw at the exit gates the religious police. Stern faced men, they held their long wooden staves at the ready waiting to clamp down on anyone who didn't shut up shop promptly for midday prayers.

The crowd was quite big but I wasn't concerned, I was swept along with it into a huge square. It was getting hot and I was being jostled, and I was suddenly jerked into alertness by the sheer numbers of people that I'd become part of. There must have been thousands, all pushing and moving inexorably towards the centre. I could see the sides of the square at first. Great huge castle-like buildings, with massive wooden doors were studded all over with iron bolts. Above, green domes and minarets, and as we passed I could glimpse a few palm trees. It was a vast sea of bobbing red chequered and white covered heads, all males, no females in sight. Dressed as I was I just blended in. It wasn't noisy, although people were whispering to themselves and each other and fingering their prayer beads. It was this that made me think that I was being carried along to a vast open air prayer session. This started a slight panic which I decided was unnecessary because if I followed what everyone else did I'd probably be all right.

Abruptly the crowd came to a shuddering, swaying halt, and it was obvious that I wasn't getting any further, neither was there room, jam packed as we were, to pray. I hardly had time to think of how to get myself out of the predicament, when I heard raised voices behind me. Heads turned and a bunch of black robed and gold braided Arabs with white head-dresses pushed forward. This was some sort of VIP group I hazarded a guess, sheiks probably, as the crowd parted respectfully and with some difficulty for them. The problem was that they surged forward, taking myself and my nearest neighbour into their midst and with them! I was really scared now and tried to edge my way out of the party but I couldn't. We moved further and further towards the centre. I became agitated and twisted and turned, I started to shout but realizing there could be a problem, kept my mouth wisely shut. Suddenly we were there at the front. It was only then that I fully understood what I was to witness.

I didn't have time to be horrified or shocked, that came later. Image followed image stamped on my mind.

A black asphalt square about fifty yards at each side. A cordon of police holding the crowd back. Neat, olive coloured pressed uniforms, knife edge creases and berets, hands clasped behind their backs. A corridor at one side of the square leading to stone steps and up to a wooden door in a prison-like fortress. Down the corridor, a line of twelve men was making its way into the square.

Every other man was a soldier, their smartness contrasting completely with their companions. These were wild looking dishevelled creatures with hands tied securely behind their backs with rough rope leashed to their captors. Their beards and hair struck me. Jet black, straggly cascades of dirty uncut and unkempt locks. They looked semi-human. No one I had seen appeared as they did, most Saudis sported smart neat goatees or were clean shaven. The wild men staggered and swayed, their eyes were vacant they seemed in a trance or drugged. My brain made a connection and flashed back to Jeddah. These men were the cause of me leaving so quickly two months ago!

The realization of what was to come caused me to try and look away. I couldn't, to the sides I could still see the scene, so I looked up. The sky was light blue, and wispy high white cumulus clouds were stationary above my head. It was the blazing sun that compelled me to turn my gaze back, it burned my eyes and forced them to seek sanctuary in front of me. It numbed the horror I felt.

Sanctuary was not available to the men. They were now kneeling in a semi-circle, swaying and twisting, shuffling their bodies like snakes but held fast. A chant went up from the centre of the square. A group of Imam were gathered together. One of them was reading out loud from a parchment. The crowd was completely quiet, many heads were bowed and most people's hands were silently fingering their beads.

The voice continued chanting, increasing in pitch until it was a whining siren echoing round the minarets. The Imam finished abruptly, and the stern faced group with him turned to the kneeling figures.

The executioners were standing behind each man. I didn't notice them much, it was the swords my eyes fixed on.

The blades appeared from nowhere and stabs were made in the sides of the swaying flesh. The line of kneeling victims shrieked out in pain, and in unison they arched their backs and heads. Their cries were cut off. The swords snapped and flashed in the sun. They fell together in a gleaming arc, sweeping through their victims' necks. The corpses, held by the ropes were released. They fell together, spouting fountains of blood from the severed necks. Around me I could hear the crowds' mutterings. *Insh'Allah,* it is God's will.

A long time has passed since that day. The rational side of me accepted and still does what I saw. It wasn't barbaric, medieval or uncivilized. Every creed after all has its swords. This was Islamic justice. To please Allah, defend the sanctity of the Holy Ka'aba and his worshippers. That I understood and respected. It's the emotional part of me that can't come to terms with it. Despite time, friends and help. It's the triggers you see.

A glint of sunlight in a car mirror. The jerk of two or three heads in a crowd. My mind locks on that day. Pools of blood flooding the black asphalt. The kneeling figures drift across my horizons, swords stab my dreams.

I didn't take the head-dress home. When I was able to move to the edge of the square I took it off and left it there where it belonged and I didn't.

The Trains
───Still Run On Time───

I LEFT THE flat for the last time that summer and made my way down to the beach. This was a ritual that I had followed every holiday over the previous five years. We always split the long school vacations into two. Rosa, my Italian wife, would take the children off to our apartment by the Adriatic just outside Ravenna, I'd join them for two weeks, fly home and then when they finally got back to England they'd shoot up to our other place on the Yorkshire moors and I'd join them for the last week, before the return home to Eastbourne and back to school. It made for interesting, if schizophrenic, summers. Byzantium and Brontë, the kids used to say.

I was about to make the transition that summer before catching the bus, to catch the train, to catch the plane. Not having a car was one of the pluses of the holiday and a real treat for me.

The transition was an early trip down to the beach, to have a last swim, and say goodbye to our friends Vicenzo and his wife, Teresina, who owned the beach bar. I had my travelling bag with me and would change into my costume in the cabin we rented at the back of the bar. There were few people around at that time, before-seven, just a couple of early morning bathers and the owners of the various establishments putting out their umbrellas, chairs and deckchairs ready for the day and the customers. I remember waving to Vicenzo, who even at this hour, had the habitual cigarette hanging from his mouth as he raked the sand, and I disappeared to change.

The sun was an orange ball coming out of the distant horizon over the sea, as I walked past him. From the corner of my eye I could see him grinning. I soon found out why! I gazed romantically at the clear blue sea and ran straight in, diving into the cool water. I swam a few yards, stood up smiling, and then yelped. The bottom of the seabed was, I saw, screaming now madly and lifting my feet in a mad dash to get out, covered in tiny crabs. Hundreds of them, all intent, it seemed, to scramble over and up my feet and legs. I danced out very ignominiously and just heard, above my cries, Vicenzo shout, 'They'll get you, Engleesh!' Beside him stood Teresina, whom he had clearly invited out to view the pantomime. I made my way up to them.

'You might have told me,' I said. He laughed and moved his arms to gesture hopelessness in the time-honoured Italian way.

'Come and have a coffee,' he said, 'before' – and he glanced at his watch – 'you miss the bus.' I was not amused.

I changed quickly with no damage I noticed, to legs or feet, and putting the wet costume on a hook, grabbed the bag, locked the door, and went around the huts and into the bar. A cappuccino was already on the counter. We talked in Italian, which, although not fluent in, I could speak well enough.

The Italians, thank God, made allowances; if you made an effort, they didn't mind how bad your Italian was. Not like the English, who would take a perverse delight in detecting the slightest trace of an accent and remark with their superior grin 'You're foreign, aren't you?' as if it mattered nowadays. Vicenzo was generous by nature and tolerated my occasional wrong genders and literal translations from my mother tongue.

'To a good season,' I said. 'Many thanks for your hospitality, and to next year.' This always pleased him. I knew what was coming so I glanced meaningfully at my watch.

It began, the five minute speech which I and every other patron of the bar was treated to by Vicenzo, if given half a chance.

'It's not been too bad this year,' he said, 'but the world gets worse. The discipline's not there any more. These *ragazzi*,' he said, 'too much money and not enough manners.' He gesticulated to the empty bar, but I knew what he meant. It was usually inhabited with noisy youths and their girls, listening day in and day out to the reluctantly installed, but money-spinning, crowd-pulling juke box.

'In my day,' he said wistfully, 'they would have respected their elders.' Teresina snapped at him.

'Your day?' she said. 'Pooh! In your day they made the old

people do exercises, in your day they wore black uniforms.' She dismissed him by turning on her heels and storming into the kitchen behind the bar.

'Chaos,' he said. 'Now when we went into Albania we brought order!' He gestured to the wall. A faded photo of Vicenzo on his horse somewhere in Albania hung there. 'Those,' he said 'were the days. Now everyone's on strike.'

I nodded. It was best not to get into any discussion on the matter. My wife, who had only been one year old when her parents were turfed out of their house by the Germans, had warned me not to get involved. There was a picture of her in the mountains, in the arms of her mother, surrounded by rough looking peasants – most of them partisans – who'd been shot in the last days of the war. When they'd changed sides, lots of people had disappeared but there had been no Nuremburg trials in Italy. Vicenzo, it was clear to see, had been of a certain persuasion and it didn't do to stir the waters. I suddenly caught on to what he'd said.

'Strike!' I exclaimed. 'What strike?' He grinned.

'The railways,' he said. 'They can't get enough money so today they're on strike.'

I don't believe it, I thought, he's having me on. I shouted to Teresina. 'Strike,' I said. 'Is there a strike?' She heard me and rushed out, suddenly aware of my problem.

'Yes,' she said. I glanced at my watch. The bus – what to do? I'd have to get the bus, there wasn't a taxi in the village, not at this time, anyway. Panic set in. Vicenzo was grinning again.

'Hurry, English!' he said with a laugh. 'You'd better get to Ravenna and see.' I was going to frown, but thought better of it. I shrugged my shoulders.

'I'll be seeing you,' I said and turned pretty smartly to rush out and down to the bus stop. In twenty minutes, I thought, as the bus hove into view, I'd find out what was going on. Perhaps they'd just been joking. They hadn't been.

The bus driver, when I'd asked him, had confirmed it. My heart was sinking as I drew into Ravenna and leapt out just opposite the station. My heart sank again when I saw a picket line. A policeman stood by the line and I rushed up to him. 'The train to Forli,' I said.

'Trains,' he said, 'no trains,' and gestured to the twenty or so crowd behind him. 'Twenty-four hour strike.'

'The bus, is there a bus to Forli?' He looked at his watch.

'The bus to Forli. Yes' he said, 'it left half an hour ago.' No there wasn't another until midday. Taxi, I thought.

'Taxi,' I said. He gestured to the rank.

'They are not allowed here today.'

'What!' I screamed. He pointed again to the unruly looking mob behind. 'They won't allow them here.'

I didn't believe it! I only had three hours and if I didn't make the flight I couldn't transfer the ticket. Charters didn't allow for strikes. You paid the cheapest price and took your chances. My luck was running out! I went across the road and stood beside the bus stop trying to think of a solution, and there wasn't one. Outside the station the pickets were smoking, and joking, and waving their banners. The policeman was talking to an old gentleman and I was despairing. It was then that I saw that the policeman and the old gentleman were making their way towards me. The policeman stopped a few yards off and pointed at me. 'This is the man,' he said. The old man, a distinguished gentleman by the look of him, stood in front of me. He put out his hand and much to my surprise he spoke in impeccable English, but with a clipped accent. 'In a spot of bother, I understand, young man.'

My surprise showed in raised eyebrows and a very English riposte, 'Actually I am, rather.'

He was probably about seventy, I thought, though he carried it well. Stiff, lean figure, very erect, with a light brown summer suit well-cut, and a rather sporty shirt and bow tie, of all things. He was also wearing in the heat a pair of white kid gloves, one of which he now removed to extend a hand towards mine. We shook. 'At your service,' he said. 'Captain Machione,' and bowed slightly towards me. 'I heard from the policeman that you are missing your train because of them.' He glanced contemptuously behind him at the crowd in front of the railway station. 'It is not what we would want to happen in our country. I think, however,' and he smiled, 'we may be able to help. Please, what time do you have to be at Forli?' I explained. He glanced at his watch. 'Yes,' he said, 'I think that would be all right with the Signora.' I looked puzzled. He was searching for a word, he found it. 'An elevator.' I looked blank. 'An elevator,' he said 'to Forli.' I cottoned on.

'Yes, yes,' I said, 'a lift to the airport.' He smiled to

himself.

'Too many years ago, you know, my English. Please to come with me.'

As we walked, he gestured to a hotel just visible down the road and talked. 'Here every year we gather for a reunion. Many of us, all from the army, old comrades and new. We gather today. It is very important to us.' I was led into the hotel lobby. He motioned me to sit down on a couch by the entrance. 'I will return when I have her permission. If all goes well you will get your,' and he smiled, 'lift to Forli.'

Amazing luck, I thought, if it came off, and nothing lost if it didn't. I looked around the lobby. There were about seven or eight people about, all male and all of venerable age. They all had one thing in common, I noticed after a while. Straight backs. Probably all military types. I could just see off the lobby the dining room, and it was obvious that there were many more similar types having breakfast seated in the room. At its far end I could see some flags and banners draping the wall. I got up and walked over to get a better look and was standing in the doorway, when the old Captain returned. He beamed. 'I have,' he said, 'secured permission for you to ride with the Signora. She will be leaving in a few minutes. She bears you no ill.' I thanked him.

Ill will? I thought, he must have got the wrong words again. He saw where I had been looking. 'Yes.' He drew himself up. 'The reunion, every year, although,' and he made a gesture, 'there are fewer of us each time, we enjoy ourselves the same.' He had a faraway look in his eye and muttered to himself. 'Good times.'

He grabbed my arm. 'The car should be arriving. Please you should be in the car, when the Signora enters.' He pulled me over to the door and as if on cue I could see a very sleek black limousine drawing up in front of the hotel. It must be a Mercedes, I thought, as all Italian cars were very small. He took me out to it. He then had words with the chauffeur who didn't, from his looks in my direction, seem very keen on this extra guest. However, he finally shrugged his shoulders and shook the old man by the hand. Did money change hands, I wondered? The chauffeur opened the door to the front seat and my old gentleman ushered me in. I started to thank him profusely, but he held his hands up and shook his head. 'It is nothing,' he said, and glanced towards the station. He shook his head. 'We do not want you upset by that rabble.' He glanced contemptuously across again. I clasped his hand. 'They will come soon. *Bon Viaggio.*'

I sat back and watched him disappear. I glanced behind and saw that there was a glass partition between the front seats and the back. A sound of applause came to my ears, and looking out, I could see a number of the old gentlemen outside the hotel doors. They were in a line either side of the entrance, politely clapping their hands as an old woman in a black veil and coat was escorted firmly but gently by the chauffeur through their ranks. This must be the Signora, on her way to Forli, my deliverer and saviour, and by the looks of pleasure and admiration on the faces of the spectators, a very venerable personage indeed.

She was settled into the back seat of the car, a rug put over her knees. The window was slightly tinted so I couldn't see too well, and there was no recognition from her of the fact that I was there. The chauffeur got in and without a word to me, we were off.

The roads leading out of the town were familiar and I was just congratulating myself again on my good luck, when we started to leave the motorway and turned off onto a small side road I didn't know. It suddenly struck me how incongruous the situation was, and I wondered whether in fact we were heading for the airport. The thought passed through my mind that perhaps it had all been a hoax, and in fact I was being kidnapped – an all too frequent experience in Italy. The chauffeur obviously could see my worried expression. He spoke not in English, but with a heavy southern Italian accent.

'Don't worry,' he said. 'We've plenty of time and the Signora does not like the new roads. Every year she makes this journey and we go the old way through the towns they knew.' I glanced in the mirror and indeed saw that the old lady had moved over to the side and was looking quietly through her veil at the flat countryside. The driver spoke again. 'You were very lucky to have met the Captain, the Signora respects him. There were some who did not like the idea of giving such a person a lift. But the Captain insisted. It was right,' he said, 'In view of the inconvenience you have been put to by the Reds.'

'Reds?' I said. He looked at me with an amazed expression.

'Yes, that scum at the station. They still cause us problems, and yet they are tolerated.' He raised his voice on the last syllable and I could see his hands grip the wheel tightly. 'Today,' he said, 'today they chose deliberately.'

Today, I thought hard, what was so special about today? He didn't say any more. I racked my brains but couldn't see what he was getting at. I gave up and settled back to look at the countryside. It wasn't that inspiring, just flat alluvial plains, well cultivated with fruit and vines. This area had been prosperous since Roman times, quiet, cut off in a way, just farmers in isolated communities, with the sun and good soil and plenty of water, prosperous. The small villages we were passing through obviously held memories for the Signora because I could see dimly in the mirror that she would lean forward every now and then and look out it seemed wistfully. I glanced at my watch. Plenty of time. We were going to make it. I smiled inwardly and warmed to my luck, the Captain, the Signora, the chauffeur and Italians and Italy generally. I dozed and remembered the past two weeks fondly.

We were coming into Forli. It was an undistinguished town on the plains, an agricultural and commercial centre but with, I noticed, very well laid-out, if pre-war, architecture. I must have been looking intently because my companion spoke again. 'We are here again. Every year,' he repeated, 'the Signora comes to visit her husband.' I started.

'Her husband,' I said, 'he lives here?'

'You do not know?' he queried. 'The Captain did not tell you?'

'No, nothing.' He shook his head. We drew over to the side of the road.

'Here,' he said 'you can catch a taxi to the airport. We go the other way to the place.' It was getting too enigmatic for words. I opened the door.

'Thank the Signora,' I said, and then added 'and her husband.' The chauffeur looked at me horrified, and then remembered that the Captain hadn't told me.

'He is dead,' he said. 'We go to his grave for the Signora to see him. He would not have tolerated what you have had to endure, what we all have to endure today.' I looked quizzical. He leant over and pulled the door. 'When he was alive all the trains ran.' It clicked. The car pulled away. I thought, not only had he got the trains to run, but I also remembered that they always ran on time!

Sugar Daddy

SUSAN WAS BORED, glass in hand, staring out of the window on to the long green lawn to the gazebo in the distance amongst the trees. She sighed deeply, turned around and looked into the room. Susan knew that, on the mantelpiece, was the large embossed card.

The distance between it and her was comforting. She looked again, her eyes seeking it out past the Queen Anne wing chairs, and past the Chesterfield couches that flanked the old Victorian fireplace. There, next to the antique French clock that Gerald's grandmother had left them, the card stood upright and not very inviting. Susan walked across the room and picked it up, putting her glass in its place at the same time.

It was not an invitation really, it was a summons, like all the others, a command to be obeyed. Would the Lord Mayor of London send the livery men to get her if she disobeyed? She smiled for one moment. A flicker of rebellion stirred in her imagination. Yes, she thought, I'll refuse to go, then there will be consternation at the Court of the Lord Mayor. What would they do? An unheard of snub!

Susan fantasised about bewigged Sheriffs hastening from the Mayor's chamber to inform the guards, consternation on their faces, and then the scurry as they prepared the warrant for her arrest. She saw herself torn from her home by a posse of officials and confined to the Tower of London for her impertinence. The gossip columnists would have a field day. She, a Lady, the wife of one of the most distinguished City of London financiers. Why if it hadn't happened, they would say, perhaps she could have been the next Lord Mayor's wife! The clock struck five and abruptly chimed her into reality. No more time for day-dreaming.

Gerald would soon be home. The invitation said seven o'clock at the Mansion House for dinner at eight. The Worshipful Lord Mayor requests your attendance. She had better get a move on. Back to the twentieth century. She went upstairs to dress, the invitation firmly grasped in her hand.

Gerald was home. She had heard him slam the front door while she was in the shower, and he called a cheery greeting while she was drying herself. He had then gone to the other bathroom to soak and sing while she continued her toilette.

Susan loved Gerald but she was fed up, and he didn't want to talk about it. When she tried to broach the subject all he would say was that she missed the children.

Of course she missed the children. Things had changed.

When Gerald had been making his way in the City, it had been different. He was enjoying the cut and thrust of climbing the corporate ladder and she had been content to look after the family. Content no, more than that, she reminded herself, deliriously happy; they both adored their children. They had four: two boys and two girls, nicely spaced out. For sixteen years until the last one had gone to boarding school, the house had echoed with the constant sound of their laughter. Even when they were all away, there were the holidays to look forward to. She had been pleased then that Gerald was doing so well, and had seen the entertaining they had had to do, as just a very small part of their family life. It was only now, in the last three years, with all of them finished at university and two already married, that time had begun to drag, and the functions had become a bore.

The thought dragged her rudely into the present as she opened the wardrobe to choose her dress for the evening's performance – for that was how she viewed these events now. Susan stared at the rows of dresses; it was difficult to remember what she'd worn to the last Mayor's banquet. She shouted down the corridor to Gerald. His reply confirmed her worst fears. It was most of his livery company who were dining tonight, so the dinner would be packed with a lot of their friends. She wouldn't want to wear something they'd already seen! She fingered the row of clothes, her eyes finally settling on a long golden dress with sparkling threads woven through it. No, she hadn't worn that one before. She'd remembered that she'd got it from her daughter-in-law, who had said that it was rather old-fashioned for her but (she remembered her grin) would do for an older woman. She hadn't been offended and had taken it away. It was a bit sparkly, but it would make a change.

Susan peered into the dressing table mirror and saw tired eyes and an uninterested gaze reflected back. She started to make up her face and drifted away again. Wouldn't it be nice, she thought, to disappear! To turn the car around at the junction to the airport and dash away on a plane, away to sun, excitement, a trip to break the routine. Susan grimaced; trips had their dull moments. Last year they'd been to Australia but it was purely business. They got three of four invitations a year like that. Lovely places, lovely hotels, the Palace in St. Moritz, the Gritti in Venice, but it was the same old people going with them and the same old routine. Gerald would make a speech addressing the conference or meeting, and she would be taken round the town by a hired guide. They'd meet up in the evening for dinner with other couples, and the inevitable business table talk would follow. She ached for real freedom to go where she wanted, and do as she pleased. She brushed her long blonde hair slowly and leisurely to its full glorious length, and it shrouded her musings.

They met in the hall, Gerald glancing nervously at his watch. Susan with the invitation in her hand. It was a warm evening, so she took just a small mink wrap and threw it over her bare shoulders and plunging bejewelled neckline for the short walk to the waiting Bentley. Gerald was already at the wheel. They swung along and out of the drive, past the Grand Park with Windsor Castle standing out in the bright summer's evening light. They could usually make the journey into the City in just under forty minutes on a Friday, and that was about all, she glanced at her watch, the time they had. A gentleman and his lady, she thought, going to the ball. She looked in the mirror and settled down to her own reflective company.

They'd long left the motorway and were only a few minutes from the City when it happened. They had turned from the Thames embankment and along the road leading to St. Paul's Cathedral. Whether it was the evening sunlight flashing on the windscreen or whether Gerald was not looking, they would never know. Suddenly Gerald braked hard, the car screeched to a halt and they were thrown forward in their seats. They had nearly knocked someone down. They'd stopped with inches to spare. Gerald wound down the window quickly. She held her hand to her head and shook a little. She peered out to see what had happened. A young man who had been thrown almost across the bonnet, a bearded student type, picked himself up and rushed to the side of the car. He thrust his face through the window into

Gerald's. She held her breath and stared across at him, still in shock, waiting for the outburst to come.

Later that evening Susan stood smiling at everyone around her. Gerald and she were the centre of attention. She was suddenly very happy, very content. She waited eagerly for the reaction as Gerald told their story yet again to yet more people. In fact, there didn't seem to be anyone at the banquet, including the Lord Mayor, who hadn't heard about it, or wouldn't! A Cheshire cat grin crept across her face. Gerald was just getting to the punch line. She turned to the hushed and expectant group gathered around them. The evening had turned out to be a performance after all, but not quite as she had imagined it earlier.

'Then it was most, most extraordinary,' Gerald was saying. 'This bearded youth looked hard at us both, stared across at my wife, pointed, looked back at me and shouted at the top of his voice, "You should be ashamed of yourself, Sugar Daddy!" and turned and ran away!'

She sat back to bask in the approbation and thought contentedly about all the invitations that they had accepted and all those yet to come!

Preserving The Past

THE CHURCH BELLS rang out, echoing across the valley. From the village houses, families made their way slowly down the narrow cobbled streets to Mass. For ages, this process had repeated itself every Sunday at nine. The faithful paying their respects. Once, it had been a ritual deeply ingrained in the peasants' lives. Their ancestors had farmed this remote alpine valley in northern Italy, making some sort of livelihood for hundreds of years. It had been for all of that time a very hard life, just the vineyards, some grain, chickens, cows, rabbits. They had scraped an isolated existence.

Life now, however, was different. Just ten years ago the roads had come. The age-old ritual was now becoming just a habit, still maintained by the old, but dropped quickly by many of the young, who had found better things to do on a Sunday. For with the roads had come people and opportunity. The village was no longer an isolated community; the inhabitants had found that there were other ways of earning a living than just subsistence farming.

The expanding motor industry in Turin was only two hours away by bus. There were many young men, who rather than work from dawn to dusk on the farms, preferred to get up at the same time, sit in the warm seat, smoke, doze and talk to their friends. Then they worked an eight-hour shift and caught the bus back again. Now they had money in their pockets and weekends free and paid holidays as well. Luxury, whilst those who stayed working on the farms had very little.

Gradually, with the wages the men had brought home, things began to change, cars were bought, houses done up and even a hotel opened for the new weekend visitors from Milan. The city dwellers drove up to walk in the unspoilt woods and mountains surrounding the village. The villagers were no longer alone.

The visitors parked their cars in the village and bought rolls, wine and ham from the shops and then picnicked in the hills. Some farmers sold off parts of their land so that houses could be built, for the richer businessmen who wanted weekend cottages. Others sold off parts of their houses that had been in their family for generations, the Milanese were only too pleased to buy the rooms at the top of a house and modernize them for summer retreats. In this way, many of the villagers prospered and made new lives for themselves. But some of them didn't.

One such family that had not shared in the changes were the Albanis. Perhaps it was because they were on the outskirts of the village, in a small hamlet of just five houses, all owned by them. Or perhaps it was because they were deeply attached to the surrounding farm that they had had for the last hundred years. The Albanis kept themselves to themselves, and although they were accepted amongst the villagers, there was nevertheless a distance between them.

It was rumoured that they weren't even Italians, but French and that one of their ancestors had been a soldier of fortune with Garibaldi when he had unified Italy. It was said he'd cashed in his spoils and used them to buy the farm. He'd married a local girl – after all, who could blame her family, with such poverty around, a man with a farm was a catch! Then he'd changed his name to Albani, and their descendants had been farming the land ever since.

There was Signor Albani, the founder's grandson, and head of the family. He was eighty years old but as strong as an ox, and still doing his share in the fields. His wife had been dead for over fifteen years. Their only son had married young but then had been lost in Russia in the war, his wife had remained on the farm, and it was she who now looked after the house. The three sons of that marriage had been brought up by their grandfather and lived and worked in the fields under his stern eye. The two eldest of them had, as soon as they could, married local girls, sired children, and their offspring now roamed about, doing their part as bidden by their fathers or the old man.

Apart from Mass on Sundays, when the whole group presented themselves at the Church, the Albanis were hardly ever to be seen in the village. Almost self-sufficient and living simply, they sat in the evenings, had their meals round the old kitchen table, talked of crops, tomorrow's jobs and never for one minute looked at what was going on around them. This was life as they had known it for years. Even the children who went to the local school and were more exposed to the things happening in

the village, kept themselves to themselves, and all of them looked forward to leaving at fourteen and working full time on the farm.

The youngest son had also married recently, but his wife came from a village far away across the mountains. She was not what the villagers would call a local girl, and she was different from the rest of the family in her outlook as well.

In a way she was more modern, and while content to remain with her husband, did not like the way all the family kept themselves to themselves. She wasn't used to it.

Her name was Maria. She was young, nineteen when she married, strong, and stocky, she had blonde hair, fine features and sparkling blue eyes. She had met her husband through her father's business dealings with the grandfather. Her family were farmers as well, and she had been attracted to the strong, silent young man who began to court her, visiting her every Sunday for a year across the valleys. They hadn't known each other very well, but when he had asked her father for her hand, she said yes. It seemed the right thing to do. Her mother had wed that way and seemed happy. They married, she moved to the farm, and for a while she had enjoyed the new scenery, welcoming family, and the change it made, but then she began to feel lonely.

Maria didn't know anyone outside the family, except for an old school friend Valeria, who had also come from her village and married another local young man, the shoemender, Pierino. Valeria had a completely different life from Maria's. Her husband, Pierino, was a good example of the village's new mentality. A sharp modern man, he had taken advantage of the influx of the weekend and summer visitors by converting the cobbler's shop into a small bar.

It had been hard going at first, but gradually a regular clientele had been established and then a thriving business. With the money earned Pierino had gone into property development, buying up some old village houses and even a stable, and renovating them to let out during the summer. They really were doing very nicely now, the epitome of the new local entrepreneur. Pierino had bought a new car, they had two young children who were always well dressed in the latest fashions, and for Christmas he had given Valeria a fur coat. Something which the older village women, including Maria's mother-in-law, tut-tutted about when she wore it to Mass in the cold winter months, but which the younger wives, including Maria, regarded with envy.

Maria saw Pierino's and Valeria's success and envied their lives. She started to nag her husband, gently at first, then more persistently, trying to get him to do something more with his life. Pointing out Pierino's success she tried to persuade him to take a job in Turin but to no avail. He was stubborn like all the Albanis and preferred working on the farm. Maria began to become more and more discontented. Resentment began to gnaw away at her. The family began to get on her nerves.

When she failed to get a response from her husband or anyone in the family to her problems, and began to have arguments with him, she took to long absences during the day visiting Valeria in the bar. She began to neglect the family duties assigned to her, and longed for some variety to distract her from the familiar routines. A distance grew up between her and the other Albani wives.

This went on for some time until Pierino, who could plainly see her boredom, asked Maria if she would like to work in the bar – Valeria was pregnant with her third child, and finding the work heavy. If she could come, then well, it wouldn't be forever, but if business did keep up, then possibly it might be a permanent job. The pay, well that wouldn't be a lot – 150,000 lire a month, but it wasn't hard work. She was already helping out whenever she visited them.

Maria couldn't believe her good luck, she was delighted, accepted immediately and went straight home to tell her husband, thinking how happy he would be. Now they would be able to save some money for a car she told him and well, the local town was nearby and they could go and visit it, many horizons could open up for them. Her husband heard her, shrugged his shoulders and said he'd discuss it later.

That evening at dinner the whole family was gathered round as usual. The patriarchichal head, the old man, stared coldly at her when his grandson told him what Maria was going to do. There was silence, no one said a word, everyone continued eating the meal, chewing their food slowly, but all looking at Maria, who although bursting with happiness inside, kept a straight face. She didn't really want to offend her family – they had been good to her, it was true – but she was taking this job. They would soon see after a while what a difference it would make. She day-dreamed

73

and ignored the family's cold reaction. The money wasn't everything, she thought. She would be able to tell them about the people she had met. The youngsters from the town on their motorbikes, the hunting parties that came for a day's shooting. The rich Milanese, who had bought the new apartments on the hill. Yes, they'd all see what changes it would bring. She cleared up with the other women and didn't notice the raised voices of the men, arguing outside on the terrace with her husband.

Maria didn't appear at Mass the next Sunday, although the rest of the family was all there. A day later, the grandfather and grandson called at the bar and asked to see Pierino. They spoke for just a few minutes, and after the discussion Pierino called his wife over and explained that Maria couldn't take the offer of the job after all. She had fallen ill and was just not available. Valeria pressed her husband for more information but he shrugged his shoulders and told her to forget it. That was the Albanis' affair, not his.

Valeria was worried. She asked Pierino to go down to the farm to see her. Why should he, he said to her again. The Albanis' business was their business. He was also smarting inwardly from the grandfather's rebuke to him for offering Maria a job. What can you expect from such people, he thought. They had no idea how things worked now. That was their loss. He was doing nicely, thank you.

On Sunday Valeria asked the parish priest about Maria's illness but he also knew nothing and did not want to get involved. Valeria wanted to go down to the farm herself but as she was near her time and the farm was isolated well away from the main roads, it was an impossibility.

She continued to nag Pierino about it and after two weeks he finally agreed that he'd visit the farm. Valeria gave him some strong tonic wine to give to her friend and urged him to go that Saturday, but reluctant to lose his weekend trade, Pierino left it to late on the following Monday.

He shut the bar at 7.30 and set off moaning to himself and wondering what kind of reception he'd get from the dour and in his opinion, backward Albanis. He left his car by the main road and began the mile long trek down a narrow dirt track to the farm in the valley below.

Halfway down he got caught in one of the sudden thunderstorms common at that time of year. He saw the barn which the

Albanis used to keep their winter fodder just fifty metres in front of him and ran for cover in the driving wind and rain.

He stumbled in front of the old broken down building's doors and pushed his way in. He stopped to catch his breath and then his nose wrinkled suddenly with disgust as a loathsome smell filled his nostrils. Suddenly the barn door crashed open behind him, pushing him further into the gloom. A flash of lightning lit up the interior. He screamed. A body was swinging in the blast of wind from a beam in front of him. What was left of Maria's bloated face looked down, grinning hideously in death through the noose the Albanis had hung around her neck.

Not Quite
—A Conquistador—

I'D MISSED the connecting flight to Mexico City at Madrid Airport by some ten minutes. I'd had an hour between arriving from London to get it, but then hadn't counted on the delay. It was infuriating, as I prided myself on being the cleverest of travellers. My time-saving rule had let me down. The rule which I had evolved many years before, was never to arrive for a flight more than twenty minutes before it was scheduled to take off. This was contrary to the airlines' instructions to arrive at least one hour before. My way you avoided the tedious queues, and provided you travelled with just hand baggage, you were ushered straight through.

The theory was that you saved enormous amounts of time and only ran the occasional risk of missing one or two flights. On balance over a year it was a winner. The let-down, of course, was that it failed to cater for late take-offs and on this occasion, the fog in London. It also engendered a false sense of being in control of what was really uncontrollable. That was the position now. I was stuck in Madrid, and checking up on the next direct flight, found that it wasn't until the following morning. An unexpected twenty-four hour delay.

Never mind, get yourself together, I thought. I knew my way around Madrid and what to do. Re-establish control. Manage the situation. Be positive. I grinned inwardly about taking the lessons that I was paid to impart to others, to myself, in a crisis management situation. I wasn't the company's star management trainer for nothing you know.

On the way back to the airport the following day I was feeling pretty pleased with my performance against my objectives of the night before. I'd phoned a local colleague I knew and he'd booked me into the nearest hotel to his home and collected me that evening. We had a great dinner and chatted over the assignment. I was off to train a number of our managers from the Mexican operation, at the invitation of the local Senior Vice President.

Mike, my Spanish colleague, had been disparaging about them for some time. Summarized, his views were 'lazy people who never did anything right'. He adopted what could only be described as an imperialistic approach to anyone, it seemed to me, who hadn't been born in Madrid, let alone Spain. He only seemed to tolerate me as a representative of the English race because we had at one time, like the Spanish, had an Empire. It was clear that he still viewed the Mexicans as being part of the original Spanish conquest. I'd neatly turned his rambling conversation on the subject to other things before he got on to his old hobby horse of Gibraltar. We parted the best of friends and I returned to the hotel and bed, and slept like a log.

There was, I decided, as I boarded the flight the next morning, a delicious sense of freedom in missing the plane. A day all to yourself with no schedule to be followed. The piper, however, had to be paid, and I settled down to the journey with a good book and a Scotch on the hour. As the boredom of yet another international flight overtook me, I watched the movie, which wasn't very good. As an afterthought I looked through my notes for the programme. Time management, setting priorities, objectives. Courses that I had run for years and years across most of Europe and some other parts of the world, but it was my first time in Mexico. I thought about all the places I'd been and drifted off to sleep.

I was still dozy as we came in to land and I struggled off the plane and into the reception buildings. That was the start of my troubles. Customs took an hour to clear! Chaos reigned supreme! Laid-back wasn't the word for it. The officials, if you could call them that, lived up to the myths created around them in some old Hollywood films I'd seen. Dirty caps on greasy heads, dishevelled khaki uniforms, smoking thick, pungent local cigarettes. They gave desultory glances at our luggage and I noticed, only paid any interest to the younger girls going through. These choice specimens of youth's baggage was assiduously searched.

It was hot and I was sweating profusely and agitated as I emerged into the mêlée of people that was my first introduction to Mexico. I walked around a bit but could see no one with what I

77

had been promised would be a card with my name on it, and transport into town. The crowds got thicker as more and more flights seemed to disgorge their passengers. I pushed through the people and into a less busy area. There was obviously no one to meet me. I felt a sudden tug on my sleeve.

'Taxi, Senor? Taxi?' I turned to see a well-dressed young man holding on to my arm. I tried to shrug him off. 'Taxi to town, Senor?' he repeated. I hesitated and that was my downfall. My case was swiftly grabbed and I followed the beckoning arm wearily. I only had time to shout out my destination – the Hotel Melior, and followed cursing my hosts under my breath.

Christ! I said to myself. You'd have thought that someone would have sent a taxi to get me. After all, I had sent a telex from Madrid, explaining the delay. All this way, and me, the Vice President for Training and Development in Europe, the least they could do. Bloody slack, I called it. I'd really make them pay for this.

I'd made a mistake. We weren't going to the taxi rank, we were heading for the car park. You fool! I cursed myself, the old trick! And I'd fallen for it. This wasn't one of the regular taxi drivers, it was what we called a 'fly by night'. One of the touts that can be found at any airport in the world. I, the experienced inter-national traveller, supposed to know his way around! I, of all people, had got hooked. I looked up but my Mexican was way ahead of me, walking fast, bobbing and weaving across the crowded road and only glancing occasionally behind him to beckon me on and I had no choice but to follow!

We stopped in the middle of a dusty car park some way from the main terminal and by a big American Buick which also looked as if it had come from an old Hollywood film. My bag was already in the boot and the door was being held open for me. I was trapped. I made a hopeless gesture to get the situation back in control.

'Por favor,' I croaked, 'Quanto est?' That was the sole extent of my Spanish. 'Poco,' came the reply, I gave up and shuffled into the back seat. The rearguard action hadn't worked. Then I had another shock, for sitting deep in the front seat, hardly visible, was a young girl. What was happening? What had I let myself in for? It was too late to do anything. We were off. The girl turned and smiled at me briefly. Ominously, I thought. Panic set in. Smiling, perhaps, before my throat was slit. All the self-assuredness I ever had, vanished. I was really scared. Visions of being robbed and murdered crept into my brain. Who would know? Just another statistic. Abducted to one of the slum areas I'd heard about. They would probably pull over soon. My whole life started to flash in front of me. Suddenly the girl turned right around. This was it, she pulled herself up onto her knees and looked me full in my worried face.

'The Hotel Melior,' she said, 'isn't very far, and my friend is a good driver.'

I felt a complete fool. I spluttered my thanks and sank into the back seat and breathed a sigh of deliverance. What an idiot I'd been. She spoke perfect English without a trace of an accent.

'I hope you don't mind,' she said, 'I work at one of the airport shops, and my friend' – she pointed at the youth next to her – 'always gives me a lift home. The buses are dangerous. Too many pickpockets.'

'No,' I said, 'I don't mind at all.' Waves of relief were still flooding over me, and guilt. What a pretentious person I was, always ready to believe the worst of anyone.

'Would you like a cigarette?' she said.

'Thanks. But why not try one of mine?' I replied. 'Duty free,' and I handed across a packet. She took one and lit it but handed the packet back to me. 'No, keep it,' I said as if this, in some small way, would make up for my previous error of judgment.

'O.K.' she smiled, and took the packet of cigarettes and put them in her bag.

Relaxed now, I looked around me, not that there was much to see. Life wasn't so bad, after all. We were obviously coming into town. I had never been to Mexico before, as I have said, but I had read up, as was my habit, on the country.

These people or the original inhabitants, the Aztecs, had had a prosperous civilization here when we, in the European sub-continent, were just stumbling into the Middle Ages. Their capital had been on the site of present-day Mexico City. It had, I remembered, been a huge lake with many islands and causeways linked together. In the middle had been the Temple of the Sun and it had been here that the Aztecs had practised their religion. This consisted of making frequent live sacrifices on top of their pyramids, tearing the hearts from their victims, and tumbling them into the lake below to be eaten by the crocodiles. Nice people, the Aztecs. They believed that if they didn't appease their gods in this way (and they had many) that the end of the world and universe would follow. In fact, this was exactly what had happened.

Their priests were the major power in the land and it was their fault that the whole country had met its Armageddon. The priests had foretold that one day a god with a white skin and beard would return as a mortal onto the shores of the country and that this god had to be obeyed and appeased if they themselves were to maintain their civilization. So when the Spanish had turned up led by a white man with a black beard, they let the Conquistadors in and everyone now knew what had happened when they had got their hands on the gold of their El Dorado.

Looking around at the people milling on the streets, I could see that this was a hybrid nation. There were dark skinned Indians, white-skinned people looking very much Spanish, and many different colours and contrasts in between. My thoughts were interrupted by the girl.

'Why are you coming to our country?' she asked.

'On,' I said, leaning forward, 'I work for an American organization and I am training some managers who run the local business here. Tomorrow I go to the Holiday Inn at Tasco where the meeting is.'

She looked at me in amusement. 'Tasco!' she exclaimed.

'Yes,' I said. 'Do you know it?' She laughed.

'Yes,' she said. 'I know it.' She looked rather strangely at me, then spoke to her friend in Spanish. Certainly they spoke about Tasco. Her friend, when they'd finished, looked strangely in the mirror at me. The girl pointed in front, down the street.

'Hotel Melior,' she said. 'Just down there.'

'Thanks,' I replied. 'How much will it be?'

'Say, twenty dollars?' she said. I was amazed and gratified. That was really very cheap by anyone's standards. I actually gave them twenty five dollars because I was still feeling guilty about my initial reaction to them. They both shook hands and I waved goodbye. Just as they pulled away the girl wound down the window and giggled.

'Best of luck in getting to Tasco,' she said. I grinned and waved back and went into the hotel.

The next morning I knew why they'd been amused about Tasco. I'd paid the overnight bill and was standing opposite the concierge's desk. The concierge, a small, fat man with a green uniform, was staring at me, aghast. I'd just asked him about getting to Tasco.

'Senor,' he said. 'Do you know where Tasco is?' I took out the travel arrangements I had been given by my secretary. Plane to Madrid. Connecting flight Mexico City. Overnight at the Melior Inn. Holiday Inn, Tasco, six nights.

'I thought it was a suburb of the city,' I said to the concierge. He stared, unbelievingly, at me. He turned to the map of the city plastered on the wall behind him.

'Tasco, Senor, is that way' and he gestured to the top right of the map. 'In fact, Senor, it is ninety miles that way.' It was my turn to be horrified.

Those bastards, I thought. Those sons of bitches! They'd asked me to come all the way out here, then not turned up at the airport to collect me and then not even informed me that the location for the seminar was ninety miles away. Another set back.

'How do I get there, then?' I asked the concierge. 'Plane? Train? Bus?' He replied to all this shaking his head vigorously.

'No Senor, it is Sunday. No planes, no trains' – and he glanced at his watch – 'and you've missed the bus. No, Senor, the only way for you to get to Tasco is to get a taxi, and you'd better leave straight away because today there is a football match and there will be heavy traffic out of the city.'

I could have cried. I railed in my mind against the world and this conspiracy of fate, my office, the head of the company in Mexico, and everyone else; but above all myself, more than anything else, for being so stupid as not to have checked up on the detail. It couldn't get any worse, I thought. I sighed and looked at the concierge. 'Call me a taxi,' I said, resignedly.

It couldn't get any worse, I had thought, but it did. The trip was a nightmare and I am going to spare the details. It wasn't the fact that the traffic was chaotic, as the concierge had so rightly predicted. It wasn't that the taxi was old, beat-up and that the driver didn't speak a word of English. It wasn't even the fact that we chugged along at just fifty miles an hour on the highway (if you could call it that). It was just that it was five hours of sheer hell!

We passed crowded suburbs, slums, farmland, scrub, semidesert. We stopped once for gas and even then the coca-cola machine didn't work. I was too exhausted to worry, past caring, I just wanted to get there. At last we saw a sign 'Tasco'. We wound up a curving road to the top of a mountain and the Holiday Inn, Tasco. We'd made it. I glanced at my watch. Three thirty. Salvation was at hand. I stood like someone who had got off a stagecoach, dusty, hot, shirt and trousers soaked in sweat. My case was out of the boot and I was paying off the driver. One hundred and twenty US dollars was the agreed price and it was about all I had. The concierge back in Mexico City had cleared his cash desk out for me and certainly the exchange rate I had paid him was way over the top, but 'if you want to get to Tasco on a Sunday. . .' he had said, and gestured helplessly as I had changed my traveller's cheques.

I waved feebly to the driver and made my way into the lobby. No one was at the desk so I rang the desk bell and waited, wearily. After a few minutes and no response I rang it again. Still no one came out. I left my luggage and went round to the back of the desk and gingerly opened the door marked 'Manager'. There was nobody there either. I walked back to the lobby and saw someone, a waiter(?) moving in the dining room. He spotted me and began walking over. Surely, someone from the office, some of the delegation had arrived? The waiter appeared. He looked at me quizzically.

'The Manager,' I asked. 'Where is he?' The waiter pointed through the dining room to what I could see was a terrace beyond. I glanced across following his outstretched arm. At the back of the dining room were huge French windows and outside the windows, a terrace which dropped to a swimming pool. At the side of the pool, I could see, sitting in a chair in a swimsuit, bathing in the sun, a solitary person. The manager? I made my way across out and down to him. He heard me coming and turned around. I explained, wearily, that I had a reservation, that I represented a big American company and we had a training course, which according to my telex, which I waved at him, started that evening in his hotel.

'We are expecting no one Senor' he said. I couldn't believe it. What was I doing here, half way round the world and nothing was going right? Perhaps the address was wrong. I had been sent on a nightmare journey. No one in their right mind would book a hotel ninety miles from Mexico City for a training course!

Surely this was a hoax!

The manager put a bathing gown on and I could see him looking at me again with strange eyes. He probably thought I was a lunatic. I caught a glance of myself in the French windows as we walked through them to the reception desk. I didn't blame him. I certainly didn't look like an international business manager, I looked like a dirty old hippie, a relic from the 'sixties. He left me at the desk and went into his office. Three minutes later he was out with a telex in his hand and a worried look on his brow.

'You are right, Senor. We do have a booking for twenty people for one week, starting tonight.'

He suddenly straightened up. 'I will get you shown to your room.' For the second time in twenty four hours, waves of relief flooded over me. It hadn't been a mistake, I really was supposed to be here.

The manager seemed to be going mad. He was screaming and shouting down the phone and had summoned out of the blue a receptionist and a bell boy, who was grabbing at my bags eagerly. I was led off and behind me I could hear the manager continuing his hysterics, shouting instructions at about half a dozen staff that had suddenly appeared from what looked like to me to be a permanent siesta. I smiled to myself. For the first time I felt secure, cocooned in my hotel, against the world, back to creature comforts. I looked around as we walked around the pool and across the courtyard. It was beautiful; flowers, vines, trees. The sun shone as I was led up the steps to my room and I realised that it could be a good week after all.

I showered, changed and relaxed with a drink from the mini bar. I must have dozed off because I was rudely awakened by the phone. Answering it, I heard a familiar voice. It was Manuelo, my host.

'We wondered whether you'd get here,' he said. 'We expected you the day before yesterday. I sent a car for you but you weren't on the plane.' So that was it. My telex from Madrid obviously hadn't got there so nobody had known about the delay.

'Don't worry,' I said magnanimously, 'let's get started.'

The local management team was young, educated and enthusiastic. They'd all turned up on the Sunday evening, as planned, and introduced themselves very formally to me. After all the trauma of getting to the place, I had settled into a routine that I had run through many times before. All the material was familiar to me and I had gathered them all in the conference room and gone into my standard patter.

'Management is about seven key skills, four of which require specific processes, they are Planning, Organising, Leading and Controlling; and an additional two: decision-making and communication pervade all four areas. However the one skill which is neglected and is more important than any other is managing time. That above all things is what this course is about.'

I rattled on for about half an hour and then put the delegates into four groups of four and got them to brainstorm all the time wasters they had experienced in their working lives. This really turned them on. There had been a rush for flip charts and pens and within a very short time the conference room walls were papered all over with their favourite bugbears. I had had to hand it to them, they were one of the most enthusiastic bunch of managers I'd worked with.

They really bubbled. The bubbling continued into and through the first day as they were sent away into groups and time and time again brainstormed, debated and refined their thinking. I was enjoying myself and for once the course sped along. The only difficult area was lunch time, when my European habit of having just an hour for lunch was met with a delegation protesting loudly about them not getting their usual siesta. I wasn't about to give in until Rodriguez, one of the senior managers on the course, took me aside. The group watched us.

'You see, Senor,' he said. 'We Mexicans, we need our relaxation at midday. We don't work well in the heat,' and to support this he gestured around him at the air-conditioned cocoon of the conference room! 'We need a little rest, then we are ready to work.'

'Well,' I said. 'I am not so sure about that, what about the schedule?' He sighed and put a friendly arm around my shoulder.

'Well,' he said. 'On Thursday we can have a free evening. Then we take you out. We take you for your pleasure to La Huerta,' he hesitated, 'if you will allow us ours at midday.' I looked blank.

'La Huerta, what's that?'

'Ah,' he said, and took my arm and led me away from the

group. 'La Huerta is a lovely place, not far from here, where you will meet the most wonderful Mexican ladies. The boys,' and he gestured behind him, 'they need a little change after so much hard work, so we go there to relax. And you will be our guest.' Before I had any time to protest it was settled. He slapped me on the back and returned to the group. A longer lunch hour for a taste of paradise on Thursday!

I had about an hour's tussle with my conscience on the subject. 'Well,' I thought. 'I'm a happily married man, but who's to know?'

On the second day we had our two hour break for lunch. There were many knowing winks and whispered consultations in Spanish which ended with approving looks in my direction and nudges in the ribs.

'Thursday,' the whispers seemed to say. 'La Huerta.'

Day three took on a new significance. Even the chilli beans served at breakfast which my hosts ate with much relish, but which I usually avoided like the plague, seemed palatable.

That evening while they worked on an assignment I decided that I'd go into town for a walk. I piled into the hotel bus and asked the driver to drop me in town. He had nothing to do so he said he'd wait for me.

I walked all over Tasco, enjoying the exercise and change of scenery. It was a small place in the middle of nowhere but it had sprung up because of a silver mine which the Spanish had exploited centuries ago. The silver had allowed the inhabitants to build the most wonderful baroque church and this stood in the town square, casting a moonlit shadow over hordes of the population who seemed to be milling everywhere, even at that time of night. The Holiday Inn bus had parked across from the church and after an hour I made my way into it and we drove up the winding hill to the hotel. I slept like a log and the next morning, Thursday, was up bright-eyed and bushy-tailed, ready for the next session. This evening I reminded myself was La Huerta.

We worked steadily on and when the group got back from lunch I distributed my famous case study. The case study was the climax of the course, pulling together everything they'd learned into one exercise. They had to divide themselves into groups, agree a leader and work on an imaginary company situation in an imaginary country. It was an exercise designed to reinforce all the concepts and principles of the week. It was also a highly competitive exercise. This prospect was met by cheers as the groups elected themselves.

'Presentation of results tomorrow morning,' I said. They split into their syndicate rooms. That was it, I thought. I could take it easy, have a shower and prepare myself for the evening recreation. Tomorrow, feedback from the groups, draw a few conclusions, go through the week and call it a day around lunch time. I turned in for a quick nap and woke about five. I looked forward with anticipation to the evening. If there were going to be women tonight, then I'd better look the part. I gazed in the mirror and shaved slowly and carefully. I'd already laid out what I thought was the most fetching outfit that I had. Light blue trousers, immaculately pressed the day before by the maid. A tailored safari-type shirt that widened my shoulders and tapered my waist. Clean underwear, of course, and I had not just a shower, but a bath, using most of my supply of perfume so that the young lady, or ladies, I thought, wouldn't be worried.

'I am sure,' I mused, 'that they'll appreciate an Englishman in the place.' I smiled to myself. A bit of style after some of the rough locals they invariably got. A horrid thought had struck me the day before about the cleanliness and reputation of such a place. I had made discreet enquiries of the hotel manager, who had assured me that it was a wonderfully run establishment. No risks, Senor, he had said, grinning obscenely.

Brushing my hair and looking in the mirror for the ninth time, I glanced at my watch. Seven o'clock already. I'd better make my way over to the bar, have a drink and wait for the others. I sauntered over, already going over in my mind what the evening could unfold. After a bad start my week was turning out fine. The group were really learning everything they should.

There was no one in the bar so I ordered a drink and sat back and relaxed. I was daydreaming and fantasising about the type of woman that I was going to get. Would it be one of the lovely brown-skinned Indian girls, or one of the fine, high-cheekboned Spanish Mexican ladies I'd seen parading around the town the night before? It was only when I was on my third drink that I realised no one had yet appeared and it was already coming up to eight o'clock. Where were they? Not a sound from the conference room across the bar. I went over and opened the door; nobody there. Not to worry, I thought, they were probably obviously getting ready in their rooms. The night was young. I went back to my drink.

It was now nearly half past eight and still not a sign of anyone. Where the hell were they? This was pushing it a bit far! I went up to the front desk.

'Ramon,' I said to the manager, 'has Rodriguez or anyone been past?'

'No, Senor,' he said, and shrugged his shoulders.

'Get me his room, Number ten,' I said.

'There's no reply, Senor, it's off the hook.' I was starting to get bothered. What was going on? I went back to the bar. 'I think I'll give it another twenty minutes,' I said to the barman.

However, it was almost nine fifteen when I started to walk across the courtyard, past the pool and up the steps to the top floor of the apartment block. I could just hear noises coming from room Number ten, shouting and arguing. I banged on the door but no one seemed to hear. I knocked on the window and a face peered out. I pointed to the door and there was a hubbub inside. The key turned and an incredible stench of sweat rolled out into the cold night air. I barged in and looked open-mouthed at the scene. The group stood and sat, cigarettes burned furiously, and there were looks of sheer frenzied concentration on everyone's furrowed brows. Rodriguez was standing in front of the flip chart at one end of the room with a felt-tipped pen in his hand, pointing at one of the charts. He barely looked at me. I started to speak but he cut in anxiously.

'The other group,' he said. 'They are still at it, or they have finished? We are ahead, we believe. We will win, Senor.' The other people in the room nodded excitedly. I stared at them all in amazement. I turned around and closed the door quietly on the scene and then made a trip to the other rooms occupied by the second and third syndicates. They weren't difficult to find, either. The same noise, the same scenes of chaos, the same enthusiasm and commitment to the task. The evening was gone.

I dined alone that evening, cursing myself. 'Some manager,' I thought. 'Some trainer, some Conquistador.' I had forgotten to set them a time limit. La Huerta was a pipe-dream.

The Yellow Rose
———————Of Texas———————

JOHN D. MAKEN the Third hadn't got much time for Texans and unfortunately, it was obvious. He was from the East coast, a pedigree white Anglo-Saxon Protestant, a Harvard-educated Wasp with a sting in his tail and I was stuck with him. He was now in the process of berating one of his fellow countrymen for his laid-back attitude.

'Jesus, Chuck!' he shouted at his victim, 'you've had this little business for over nine months now and, if you don't achieve the numbers soon, baby, your number is up.'

I cringed for the man – poor old Charles, as I, English and London University educated, insisted in calling him, much to John D. Maken the Third's amusement.

'Look at these goddam results, the place is falling around your ass. Fire some of the bums, close down a department or two, it can't go on.'

Charles didn't move, he was laid-back about the whole thing, like everyone. Or was he? Since we'd arrived in Dallas two days before, I'd been struck yet again by just how relaxed Texans were. Everyone in town seemed to move in about third gear, compared to the fifth (and higher) that we were used to driving in at headquarters in New York.

We'd bought the company about a year ago. It made machines to dispense cash to our customers, and this was my third visit, but John's first. The operation seemed OK, as far as I could see, it wasn't losing money, just ticking over nicely. However, as soon as John had taken over the Division, he'd fired in true US style, the Texan company's president, by long distance, and appointed Charles in his place. Now he was obviously expecting him to have achieved miracles in just nine months.

'That's it, baby.' He pointed a finger at Charles. 'Three more months of this and your ass is on the line.' John got up to go. 'I'll

see you tonight,' he said to me. 'Go through the plan with him.'
He glowered across at Charles and stormed out.

'Well,' I said when he'd gone, grinning, 'perhaps we can do
some real work now.'

'Son of an Eastern bitch,' Charles muttered but smiled at me
as he said it.

An hour later I was in the cab on my way back to the hotel.
Strange, these Americans, I thought, I'd never really got used to
their ways. It was interesting, comparing management styles
around this country and the world, something I'd had plenty of
time to observe in many years of working for the International
Division.

We English were reserved, bureaucratic, had tremendous
technical creativity and inventiveness but lacked the sheer sales
drive and resources to push and exploit the ideas properly and
profitably. We tended to cope with limited resources by stealth
almost. We would prioritise and plan, while the Americans with
their bigger bucks would chuck money at things. Always go for
broke, and well, if it did go broke, you were fired and you went
elsewhere. No stigma if you lost your job here, not like in the
UK.

The Dallas Metropolis, a name conjured from, it seemed to
me, a superman comic, flashed by. I mused on. The Italians, on
the other hand, were laid-back, just like the Texans or at least
they gave the appearance of being so. And yet they had
tremendous creativity, and sheer Machiavellian intrigue got
them through. No planning but everything got done, even if was
always over budget. It seemed to me in the last analysis, it was
solely their big macho egos which drove them to achieve, they
just didn't want to lose face.

Planning made me think of the Germans. They would do
wonderful plans – stacks and stacks of them, in incredible detail.
Then they'd implement them. The trouble was, no flexibility, if it
wasn't in the original plan and hadn't been spelt out, then they
couldn't deal with it! Consequently they missed opportun-
ities.

No, the best managers were probably (although as an
Englishman it stuck in my throat to say it) the French.
Tremendous ideas, as long as they were their own, marvellous
creativity and they loved the bureaucracy of planning and
organizing. Result: perfection. That, however, was their trouble

– there's no such thing in business and they would brook no comment or criticism from anyone, particularly an Englishman, so working within an international policy was anathema to them.

I'd just have to figure out what made the Texans tick? The more I saw of them, the more enigmatic they appeared; there was something I couldn't put my finger on. They looked confident enough, they were also easy enough to deal with, but there was something in their eyes and the way they held themselves, an independence but was it also a sort of resentment? I was still puzzling when the cab drew up outside the hotel.

Oh, well, I'd get a little local culture tonight and see what I could make of them. Charles was taking John and me out for some typical Tex-Mex food. This suggestion had gone down surprisingly well with John when it was mentioned, much to my surprise, given that we were here to chew the business over, as my boss so quaintly put it. But it then emerged that Tex-Mex food was all the rage in New York, and John was anxious to taste the real thing so he could surprise dinner party guests with his on-the-ground knowledge. That was something that didn't surprise me. Without the background of centuries of European history and culture, and given the rat race that they were in, half of New Yorks' executives and their wives or girlfriends were commuters between causes, fashions and fads, each seeking to outdo the other in their knowledge, or use of, the latest in-thing from English beer to Egyptian cotton socks. I glanced at my watch as I collected the key; I'd better get a move on. I'd be meeting them downstairs in half an hour.

'Where the hell's that goddam Chuck?' John exclaimed for the fourth time in as many minutes. We were standing in the lobby of the hotel and, true to form, my companion was displaying all the merits of a senior vice-president in the organisation. This consisted of an impatience verging on hysteria if events did not conform to his time scale. He'd been a green beret and served in Vietnam and the discipline it had given him was famous. The Marine Sergeant was his nickname amongst the secretaries, and it was well deserved.

Not having been in the United States at the time of that war, I exhibited a curious detachment to the stories with which he constantly regaled me. He never ceased to tell anyone and everyone of his achievements. Actually they were real. He'd been wounded twice – once in hand to hand fighting with a female regiment of VC (and anyone who had been through that earned respect, if not admiration). A few months ago he'd collapsed at his desk and had to be taken to hospital. I'd been one of the few to visit him, and I think it was for that reason alone that he kept me on, enjoying a confidence and relationship that was the envy of many.

'Old agent orange,' he'd said, when I saw him propped up in his hospital bed. 'Sprayed the jungle with it and us as well. It's in the system and nobody knows what it does, but it flares up and bang – I'm on my ass for a week.' When I'd related that back at the ranch, as I called the headquarters, it brought gasps from the females but only wry smiles from the males on the floor.

'Hoss shit,' one of them had said. 'He was the type of bastard most of us out there would have shot in the back, given half a chance.'

I kept quiet after that. The American experience in Vietnam, in my judgment, had a few years to go before it could be looked at in perspective and its true value or otherwise worked out.

'Jesus Christ,' said John. 'Get a load of this.' I looked across as the lobby doors slid open. What I saw startled even me. In front of us was Chuck, I couldn't, given his amazing appearance, dignify him now with the name Charles. What we had in front of us was a fully fledged, all-American cowboy.

'Incredible,' was all I could mutter to John, as this western apparition made its way over to us.

'How yo'all doing, then,' said Chuck, and reached out his hand to shake ours. I'd never seen anything like it. Six feet two of real American Wild West. He was wearing a stetson with a badge and feathers stuck into the middle of the leather headband, a blue and white lapelled shirt and a red bandana scarf tied around his neck. His waist was tightly held in with a hugh buckled belt to match the headband and skin-tight yellow suede jeans clung to his legs and disappeared into enormous cowboy boots with fancy stitching. We stood stunned.

'You'all gonna have a good time tonight,' he said, as he spun two bemused blue-suited executives through the front door and into his car.

The car itself was another revelation, a custom-built Buick, it was a 1950s winged model, only seen on Hollywood movie lots, with – would you credit it – a pair of cow horns on the bonnet. Chuck was showing his true colours. I was amused, John was not. How to play this one, I thought, he was thinking and settled back to see what would happen.

I needn't have worried, we didn't need to do anything. Chuck was in his element. He regaled us all the way to the restaurant with cowboy talk. If we had wanted to reply we wouldn't have been heard above his voice, which itself could barely be heard above the Dolly Parton music blaring from the stereo system. John was too shell-shocked to do anything but stare dazedly at the figure in the seat beside him. He only opened his mouth when we got out of the car at the restaurant and then only as an aside to me.

'Goddam cowboy asshole,' he said. 'No wonder no one has been canned – probably all goddamned cowboys.'

He cheered up though when he saw the menu. The restaurant was real Tex-Mex. Sawdust on the floor and plain wooden tables, hacienda-type decor and a Mexican combo going mad in the corner. The clientele was something else. This was very much the rich Texans at play. Everyone, except us, was dressed the same as Chuck. Cowboys one and all.

The men were middle-aged and rich, you only had to look at the rings on their fingers and gold bracelets on their arms and admire the cut of their hand-made suits and boots to see that. But it was the women, or cowgirls, that really stood out. Gorgeous outfits, broad hats thrown back over what seemed to be standard long golden hair, faces that shone with no make up, just healthy, fresh tanned complexions and beautiful, sparkling eyes. Chuck could see me looking.

'Like our gals, do you, boy? We got the sweetest hossflesh in Texas here. Later on we'll hit the saloons, this is just a taster.' John, I noticed, had suddenly got interested. He was divorced and next to bawling out people he liked balling out any woman he could get his hands on.

The meal was superb, after a tequila sunrise which took my head off we tucked into tacos with beans, then enchilada and ribs. The portions were enormous.

'Americans eat,' Chuck said, 'Texans stuff,' and to illustrate the fact he pushed yet another taco into his mouth. John, after his third tequila sunrise, was looking positively benign. I was getting drunk. Chuck didn't seem to be affected at all.

93

'Come on, guys,' he said, when we'd finally finished. 'Let's get the hell out of here and two-step.' The worst, or best, I though as I lurched to my feet, was yet to come.

I was right. We were so merry on the tequila that we'd been singing cowboy songs together to the tape as we whirled around the freeway to our destination. John and Chuck were up front and had suddenly to my surprise become the best of friends. It appeared that Chuck had been in Vietnam as well, and the two were swopping stories about the Rest and Recreation haunts they'd sampled. The flesh pots, from the sound of it, of Saigon. All this, in between the choruses and shouts to other drivers of, *Gettalong Little Dogie.* It was, I thought, joining in, all I'd seen or heard about the old wild west! We drew up off the highway and Chuck pointed at a huge log cabin type building at the side of the road.

'That's it, boys, the Yella Rose of Texas.' We whooped when he said it. The trip was brightening up. John and Chuck had their arms around each other's shoulders as we hit the doors.

The Yella Rose was a carbon copy of the restaurant, sawdust and plain tables. The only difference was that instead of a Mexican combo there was a real mean-looking country rock group on a raised platform at one end. Behind them there was an enormous yellow rose painted across the wall, it must have been forty feet long. The legend entwined around it was the standard Texan greeting. 'Yawl have a good time now.'

In front of the band was an enormous dance floor and round and round the floor in one direction only spun the Texan two-steppers. It looked like a cross between a waltz and a polka, and everyone was doing it. We'd only just sat down when one of the cowgirl waitresses came up to us. She clearly knew Chuck.

'Where'd yawl come from?' she drawled, looking at our blue suits.

Chuck seemed a bit nervous.

'They's from England,' he said, gesturing to me. The cowgirl grinned welcomingly.

'What'll it be, boys?' she said.

'Three beers,' said Chuck, and a few minutes later three bottle were unceremoniously dumped on the table.

'No glasses!' I shouted at Chuck above the noise, and then wished I hadn't, as I saw around me clearly that everyone was drinking from the bottles.

'Hell no,' said Chuck and then shouted, 'I'm gonna find me a gal, and two-step.' I looked at him leap across towards a group of the girls gathered around a table not far away. He swept one of them to her feet and was off. John took off his jacket. A light I'd seen before hit his eyes and he was off to the same table.

I just sat and looked at the scene. It was amazing, I thought, this is what it must have been like a hundred or more years ago. They hadn't changed. They were all still on the frontier, Texas was cattle country, feeding the East with beef herded to the rail head. Oil had come later but the same cowboys had wild catted for that as well. Beneath the smooth, sitting-in-the-saddle, relaxed approach was the frontier man. Twenty days on the trail, then dress up in your best outfit and raise hell in town.

A hand grabbed mine. A cowgirl was looking at me.

'Yawl two step?' she said.

'Ma'am,' I replied, in my best English accent, 'I certainly do not. But,' I added, 'I'm gonna try.' We swept onto the floor to join the throng. We continued sweeping around the floor for about eight dances, and sweeping around with us I could see Chuck and John, each with a cowgirl in their arms.

The atmosphere was electric. I hadn't enjoyed myself so much for a long time. The band finally came to the end of its set and with a loud whoop and 'We'll see yawl after the show,' disappeared. My partner and I made our way back. There were Chuck and John with their cowgirls and more beer on the table. I was introduced around as the Limey, and then before we could talk, there was a great drum roll, we turned and saw on the stage a sequin-dressed compère with the biggest stetson in the place taking over the mike.

'Yawl enjoying yourselves,' he said, and we all roared our approval back. 'Wellsa, now we gotta show for yawl. The prettiest gals in Texas gonna show themselves tonight, and yawl gonna vote for them. The winner goes forward to the finals of Miss Texan Two-Step in Houston in three weeks' time. Put your hands together for the five Yella Roses.' We all stood up, shouted and screamed and hats came off and were thrown in the air. Clapping started and the door at the side of the stage opened. Out came the roses.

The dancing had sobered me up, but the heat and sheer energy being generated was getting me drunk but on a different wine. The girls paraded in front of us. They were in swimsuits

96

and were lovely. Long-legged, blonde, blue-eyed. The clapping, shouting and whistling continued and as the girls walked around wiggling their backsides, several cowboys stood on the tables and stamped their feet. The noise was deafening. Then the compère called for hush. He had some difficulty getting it.

'Now,' he said, 'whichever little lady gets the most cheers, wins,' and he jumped down off the platform to take up a position behind the first girl in the line.

'Is it to be this honey?' he said. The place exploded again; catcalls, whistling. 'Or this one?' he said, skipping behind another. He was moving round to the one in front of us. Suddenly John, who'd been whooping along with us, was up and out on the floor beside him. He was shouting, and a stetson that he'd borrowed from his dancing partner was in his hand. He made to put it on the girl's breasts. The compère drew back and the contestant put her hands across her chest. The place hushed.

I remembered what I'd been told about the Texans, they may look wild, they may like their liquor and a good time, but no one, but no one takes liberties with their women. I could see out of the corner of my eye Chuck's horrified face. He moved swiftly across the floor and, with one bound, he caught John by the shoulder, pulled him round and hit him full in the face. The crash of John's body hitting the floor was the only sound in the place. He looked up and screamed at the top of his voice, 'Damned Yankees!' Everyone roared their approval.

I rushed over to help John, realising at the same time that that was the key to the whole Texan character. They'd lost one war against the North, but were still fighting it, every chance they got.

Dutch Treat

AS USUAL the winter sky over Ouderkirk was slate grey. Johan sighed and his breath turned to a hazy cloud in front of his chapped face.

The Amstel river in front of him had wound its way out of Amsterdam, through the flat countryside past neat tidy rows of houses, forest parks and meadows, into the village. He looked at the mass of water pushing under the old hump-backed bridge and turning, unloaded his bike from its resting place by the front porch. The bike was black, and shiny and new, and on its handle bars and saddle were the three crosses of Amsterdam, and the three wavy lines which together were the insignia of the Dutch Water Board.

He shouldered his big leather work bag with the same insignia into its tanned pigskin, and pushed the bike out.

That was his life, he thought, stamped all over, official, a Polder inspector for the past sixteen years ever since he left the technical school. Then he smiled; that was he thought, maybe, until today. Today was special, the day of the interview.

He jumped onto the bike and pedalled, and pulled out into the narrow cobbled street and began whistling, which he realised he hadn't done for years. Yes, today was the day he'd been waiting for. He'd worked hard and long and had been nice to his superiors and today it could all pay off. It helped to be thought of as a nice reliable chap.

A vacancy had come up down the road in Amsterdam, an office job, much coveted in his local area. District Polder Inspector, well, Assistant District Inspector to be exact, a desk job. He smiled – no more reporting in for work at the local pumping station. No more dressing in blue overalls, no more checks on the machinery and visits to the outlying pumps in the 165 square kilometres he had to cover. No more frozen mornings, or soaked-to-the-skin afternoons. A sense of wonder took over: he was a true Dutchman, in this small country stolen from the sea, and they needed men like him in the pumping stations to keep the water level down.

Pride welled up in him and he nearly missed his usual turn off at the end of the lane. In front of him he could just see the concrete block of the Ouderkirk pumping station. It looked rather forbidding but this time he rode on past it. He'd got time off for the interview and was heading to the station to take the train into Amsterdam.

He made his way up the road for two kilometres, pedalling briskly, and then turned into the station forecourt and over to the bicycle park. Every Dutch station had one of these and he joined a small queue of fellow travellers who booked their bikes into the stores, locked them, removed their clips, and made their way hurriedly onto the platform to await the train.

Sitting on the train, he gazed idly out of the window and absent-mindedly at his own reflection. Elsa would get a surprise if she could see him now. No blue overall for him today; he was wearing his Sunday best suit. Things could be different from now on for Elsa and the children if he got this job. A lump came to his throat. It was for her that he was doing this. Then he panicked, what if it didn't happen? A cold sweat broke out. Thank heaven nobody at home knew, he hadn't told Elsa or the kids anything about it. They were always fast asleep in the mornings when he left, and today he'd hidden his blue overalls, hoping that Elsa wouldn't open his wardrobe and see the suit was missing. No, she'd be off to one of her coffee gatherings or helping out at one of the voluntary clubs that she attended on one or two mornings each week.

He loved Elsa, he worshipped her; in fact, no man could have wished for a better wife or better house manager. He didn't know how she did it. His pay as a skilled technician wasn't bad, but it certainly wasn't huge and yet they never seemed to go without. They'd been able to buy the house and new furniture, they ate out once every month, and the kids were always well dressed. She managed so well, why last year, they'd even got away to Majorca for a holiday. Yes, a real housewife. That, he thought, was the good farming stock she came from, frugal, practical, hard working.

He thought about her and counted his blessings. She was quiet and peaceful to be with and yet sometimes he could sense strong currents in her. A part she held back from him as if it was too powerful for him to share. She wore wild clothes in vivid colours most of which she made herself. He, with his staid outlook teased her about it, but she shrugged off the comments and smiled; a secret smile. He was proud of her and, even if she did keep herself to herself, he preferred it. The children came first but he followed, he thought, not very far behind. Yes, he was very lucky and he was determined as well that their marriage was something worth fighting and building for.

Sometimes he wondered why she'd married him. He'd overheard once or twice her friends taunting her about being married to such a dependable but boring husband. Old bore, they'd said, attractive girl like you, don't know why you put up with him, and then before he could hear her reply, they'd all burst out laughing. It was true about her being attractive with her neat trim and curvy figure, his mates at the pumping station always made a few jokes about Elsa. He bridled at the thought of them. Well, he'd show them now. His fierce Dutch pride took over. No ambition, that was their problem. They'd laughed when he told them he'd put in for the job, but the smiles had soon been wiped off their faces when he'd actually got the interview letter. He hadn't really expected it himself and, just to make sure, he pulled the piece of paper from his pocket.

He took the letter out of the white envelope and opened it to reveal the reassuring crest of the Amsterdam Water Board imprinted on the top.

Inspector Van Holten expects you to be interviewed for the position of Assistant Polder Inspector Grade at 9.00am on Wednesday 21st September at the above address.

Another smile of satisfaction spread across his face and he relaxed. Carefully folding the paper into the envelope and tucking it in his pocket he looked dreamily out of the window again. Then he started to think. He'd never been to an interview before, at least not since the interview sixteen years ago for his present job. What about the other candidates?

He started to worry remembering what had happened to Kees, one of his colleagues, who himself had applied three years ago for a similar post.

Put him in a corridor they had, with a long line of other hopefuls. Then they'd brought them in one by one. Six interviewers, a real panel, firing questions, left, right and centre, nearly twenty minutes grilling. Then out into the corridor to wait along with the rest of them. That was the worst part, Kees had said, the waiting until everyone had finished. Then another half hour while they deliberated, then the call in for the successful candidate. That was he said they kept you guessing. Kees hadn't got the job and had been disparaging about the whole process. Johan felt as though he should go home now. His heart sank.

The train pulled into the central station and he joined the crowds of commuters bustling off the platform, into the tunnels, and out onto the street. Despite living just twenty kilometres from the city, he rarely went there. He had been born up north, and like many people of Calvinist stock regarded the Amsterdamers and their city with some suspicion. A safety valve for the rest of the country was what the local priest in his home village had called it, with a typical Dutch attitude. Well he better get used to it if he got the job. At least he'd be indoors, and the hours were shorter than those he worked now. The pay was considerably higher as well; yes, it would be a comfortable job all right, and he'd have a position which his neighbours would envy. An Assistant Inspector in Amsterdam; that would please Elsa, and be one in the eye for some of her gossipy friends. The old bore would show them.

He put a determined look on his face and walked across the square to the Damrak striding purposefully out. At least it's not too far from the station, he thought. Just by the Stock Exchange he took a left turn over one ōf the canal bridges, glancing at his watch, nice timing, ten to nine and not far to go. He couldn't help noticing the seedy area he was walking through. This was the edge of the red light district and on every side of the street there were sex shops displaying their lurid wares, and further in the girls would be opening up shop for the day.

There it was, just on the corner in front of him, the Amsterdam Water Board office, big green doors and a Commissar standing outside checking identity cards. Probably the same gruff person who'd checked Kee's credentials when he'd come here. He mounted the steps, showed the man the letter, and was directed inside the gloomy building. An arrow pointed down a corridor and he could see at the end of it a number of benches lining the walls, and two other people sitting on them, looking up at a sign which read 'Interview Room.' This was it.

He joined them and looked intently at what was obviously the

101

competition. One was a youngster, or looked it anyway. Slim, well-dressed, wearing the same Water Board insignia tie as himself, but with a grey suit. They exchanged good mornings, and he turned to the other candidate and did the same. This man was elderly and sat hunched over in a brown dungaree jacket, matching trousers, no tie. He looked very nervous and was puffing away at a hand rolled cigarette. Johan glanced at his watch. It was gone nine – was this all there was – just the three of them? By way of confirmation, the interview room door opened and a uniformed Commissar came out with a clipboard. They answered their names as he called them off. One candidate wasn't there, hadn't even bothered to turn up. What a bit of luck. Johan started to weigh up his chances, but didn't have time to think, as the official was calling his name first. Get a grip on yourself. Solid and dependable that's what you are, so show them that. He took a deep breath and entered the room.

It was stark and formal inside, green walls, white ceiling, windows overlooking the canal and a highly polished floor. A large table covered with green baize and a chair in front of it, and behind the table three, just three, officials. He proffered his hand to each of them, they shook it uninterestedly and motioned him to sit down. The interview began.

It was over, he was sitting outside, his hands clasped tightly in front of him. One other candidate, the young man sat next to him in the same position, the other chairs were empty. It was five past ten and the last man was in.

Johan was going over it in his mind. Had he made the right impression? He'd listened carefully to the questions, some personal, some technical, some general, some specific. e'd replied consistently, not one word too little or too much. It had been a terrifying experience and he thought of how ill-prepared he'd been, but then again he had been able to answer some of the most difficult questions. He hoped he'd done well, he now really wanted this job, he'd worked so hard, he wanted it for himself, for Elsa, for the kids. But more than anything for Elsa, he realised that he needed to prove his worth to her. He sweated.

That was it, the fat man was out. He looked terrible, he didn't even stay, didn't even sit down, just turned towards the door, swore and walked off down the corridor, hate and failure in his eyes. Something had gone wrong. He turned to the younger man, they looked at each other, the young man broke the silence,

'Dutch courage,' he said grimly. So that had been it, the fat man had obviously had a few drinks to steady his nerves and they'd noticed inside. An unwritten law was that no one drinks on the job; he should have known that. Johan didn't drink. He'd tell Elsa that. She was always telling him to go out, have a drink, enjoy yourself, but he preferred to stay in, his old conservatism. His chances had improved. Would he get it? The door opened, his heart sank, the youngster grinned and went in as his name was called. Always the younger man!

Finished, he hadn't got the job, leave the worst news to last. He could hear laughter from within the room. What a fool he'd made of himself, what would his colleagues say? Solid, dependable Johan, what now? His head sank into his hands. The door opened again, he was called in.

The three men's appearance threw him off balance, they were smiling, the young candidate was nowhere to be seen. They motioned him to the chair, his mind was reeling. He, Johan had got the job after all. Van Holten was standing up, moving round to join him, slapping him on the shoulder. He didn't hear his words, he'd made it. The others were already filing out.

The Inspector shook his hands again, he heard him, his head cleared. They'd chosen him, the Inspector was saying, because of his experience, his loyalty, his good solid reputation in the district, his reliability. Too many youngsters he was saying, wet behind the ears. Practical men from the ranks, that was what they were looking for. Now he was being invited out for a cup of coffee, then he'd get the confirmation in a week. Two weeks, Van Holten was saying, and you'll be in my department.

They left together, through the big green doors, walking briskly. Johan had begun to accept it, this Van Holten was someone who valued him, it was going to be good to work for him. Johan was in a dream, the coffee shop wasn't far Van Holten said. It had really happened, he'd achieved what he'd wanted. Van Holten was rabbiting on, 'Friendly lot we are, don't work too hard, join the team, Amsterdam Head Office.' Elsa would be proud, and then he stopped.

Van Holten, who was way in front, stopped himself and turned back. Funny people, he thought, these northerners, stiff and formal. God help the department with this one. He'd wanted the younger man. Christ, if it hadn't been for that recent policy decision, that a percentage of the department had to be technicians from the ranks, he'd have got his way. Typical of this local council, left-wing to the core, they didn't know how to enjoy themselves. Now there was this new man standing on the street corner looking in the windows at the girls, as if he'd never seen them before. This one was going to be a bore, the sooner he got this over with the better. He'd probably only see him after that, once a month at the departmental meeting.

He began walking back, annoyed. What was wrong with this man? Standing there stiff as a board, gaping mouth. Johan didn't move, his gaze was fixed on the window and the girl sitting there. Elsa stared back transfixed, looking straight at her husband.